Storytale

By Kevin Jackson

175

You wrote your way for me two years ago,
So now I write my way for you to know
I'm thankful for the time you took to write.
Of course, it was your course to write the news,
But have you ever been a writer's muse?
Back then, it seemed you had your head on right;
The way you seized the trails within your eyes,
I kept in awe of your pursuit to rise;
Back then, I knew that you were something bright.
Perhaps you have what every man adores,
Perhaps no soul could shine a smile like yours,
But how'd I know? — we spoke without a sight.

Keep after dreams, no stopping when you win,
You'll show the world your shining light within.

Copyright © 2012 by Kevin Jackson

Amazon Group of Companies
CreateSpace
7290 B. Investment Drive
Charleston, SC 29418

Cover Art by Kevin Jackson with sun effect inspired by NASA's Earth Observatory Sunspot images

Jackson, Kevin
    Storytale / Kevin Jackson.—2nd ed.

ISBN-13 978-1-469-92713-8
ISBN-10 1-469-92713-6

Glossary of Unusual Terms & Names

Bidellia (bih-DEL-yuh) – Queen of Pithlyn Mass, Living Goddess, daughter of Omnerce; comes from the name Bidellia, meaning High Goddess

Cil (sil) – an illmate with Makail

compé (KOM-pey) – a friend held with high regard, like a brother

confinary (con-FAHY-nur-ee) – a prison or dungeon, holding wrongdoers

Core (kohr) – home to the condemned souls after death

deep (deep) – largest body of water surrounding masses

Dux (DOOKS) – leader of Queen Bidellia's royal committee

Dymetrice (dih-MEE-tris) – the mass separated from Pithlyn by Threatle Gap; Pithlyn's foe; it is a reformation of the word diametric, meaning opposite in beliefs, ways, etc.

Favally (FAH-vuh-LEE) – the mass west of Pithlyn, separated by Pithlyn Pass; Pithlyn's greatest friend and ally; comes from the combination of favorite ally, despite the difference in sound.

Fidelis (fahy-DEL-is) – Queen Bidellia's trusted advisor

gargentwan (GAHR-jen-TWON) – humans of northern glaci, who stand more than twenty feet tall and are very brawny with excessive strength

Glaci (GLEY-see) – the mass easterly north of Pithlyn, separated by Clatter Crest; in southern Glaci, typical humans live and are great friends with Pithlyn; north of the highest mountain range on Prodigion, gargentwans live and hold Pithlyn loyalties

Gracen (GREY-suhn) – home of righteous souls after death; Heaven

iambic pentameter (ahy-AM-bik or -ik pen-TAM-i-ter) – in poetry, a ten syllable line with a pattern of unstressed, stressed syllables, five times each line: duh DUH duh DUH duh DUH duh DUH duh DUH

illmate (IL-meyt) – a prisoner currently residing in a confinary

Indiffron (in-DIF-ron) – the mass westerly north of Pithlyn; comes from the word indifferent, meaning no opinion on the matter, or insignificant; the mass is seen as an extension of Pithlyn, simply following suit

Isnelle (iz-NEL) – Makail's mother with great powers relating to nature

Jivin (JIH-vihn) – Makail's father with great powers relating to physical ability

King Avar (uh-VAHR) – current king of Dymetrice Mass, rival of Queen Bidellia and Pithlyn.

kush (koo sh, rhyme with push, not rush) – A wooden plank used as a bed with a thin grass-filled sheet for a mattress.

Makail (muh-KEYL) – born in Dymetrice, son of Isnelle and Jivin, inherited his parents' powers, seeking to find his path.

mared (maird) past tense verb-to frighten oneself while in a dream

mass (mas) – large area of land belonging to a definite leader

obscurium – (uhb-SKUR-ee-uhm) – a black chamber within the confinary where illmates are sentenced if they disobey confinary guards' orders

Omnerce (OM-nurs) – Ruler of all, God of Gods, Queen Bidellia's father

Pithlyn (PITH-lin) – the central mass of Prodigion, ruled by Queen Bidelllia; comes from the base word Pith, meaning the essential part of something

Prodigion (pro-DIH-jee-on) – the world filled with deeps and masses; comes from the word prodigious, meaning extraordinary in size, and wonderful or marvelous

raxar (RAK-zahr) – a horse-like animal capable of enduring long distances (further described in Chapter 6)

sonnet (SAWN-eht) – a fourteen-line poem using iambic pentameter and an explicit rhyme scheme

sprilen (SPRAHY-lehn) – a large, well-decorated room, typically a bedroom, meant for one of his esteem

Threatle Gap – (THRET-l GAP) – space between Dymetrice Point and Pithlyn Point where the God of Peace ripped the land, keeping distance between the foes; water beneath the gap is called the Straits of Silony

Zyder (ZAHY-dur) – the mass easterly south of Pithlyn; an ally of Dymetrice; comes from combing to foreign words, meaning south

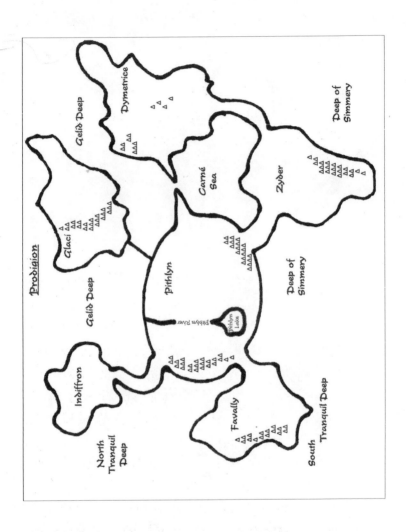

The Storm

Clear visions captured his haziest day. Dirt paths outlined the boundaries of huts. Like smoke, that dirt burst into the hot, summer air as raxars pounded along the path toward Makail's parents' hut. The common scent from his childhood of wet grass mixed with manure and soil surrounded him as he hid crouched between shrubs behind the hut across from his parents'. Feeling his heart thump faster than the booming hooves of raxars, sweat beaded his forehead, and he remained completely still except for his trembling hands.

Three raxars halted at the open door of his parents' dwelling. Two big-armed men jumped down and entered, coming out moments later with his parents tied tightly from wrist to ankle. Red besieged his father's mouth, slipping from his nose. A pinkish tone encircled his mother's right eye. They looked tired, weak. They put up no fight to convince these men of their innocent loyalties. Each of the men who seized his parents tied another long rope from his saddle to Makail's parents with no sign of reluctance or remorse while the third man on a raxar oversaw. Once the men fastened his parents to their raxars, they galloped toward King Avar's castle, dragging the captured. Makail, attempting to keep pace, raced behind huts, wishing he had his father's top foot speed.

A large crowd assembled before the execution stage. On the stage, King Avar placed himself front and center, two groups of four men stood holding spears, and rising twenty feet high from the platform were two wooden beams. The backdrop of the king's castle held withered rock formations, like tall, branchless trees as red as smoldering lava. The men who took Makail's parents untied them, hoisted them on their shoulders to carry them up for their final act, and shoved them into position against the beams. Makail painfully watched from the last row of spectators, as the groups of four men swarmed around his father to the left and mother to the right, securing each to their beam. His parents' heads were not bagged or blindfolded, for King Avar believed in letting violators stare at death closing in on them.

King Avar stated, "As a threat to the good people of my mass, these two traitors shall face the ultimate consequence! Let Dymetrice climb from fear and end the feared!" He turned quickly with both arms stretched, uttering, "now die" as he walked back to his castle. At his remark, the four on each side gripped their spears and trained them on the convicted. Synchronized, they surged their daggered edges into the chests of Makail's parents, ending the feared. With a crushed heart and quivering chin, Makail bolted away, hearing the faint voice of his mother call out to him, "Never forget our love," as he put the celebrating crowd deeper in his past, aiming toward what would become a thirteen-year visit alone in the woods of Quintix Valley.

As he awoke on a day thirteen years after the death of his parents, sunlight spilled through the eastern mountain peaks. Makail had built his home on the westernmost mountain slants on the south side of Quintix Valley. This incredible mountain arrangement formed an obtuse V, and trees covered every part of it, even shadowing a narrow river, flowing from the deep through the valley, winding between the mountains, and drifting for miles into the land. These mountains rose higher than any other mountain cluster on Dymetrice Mass, stretching more than two-and-a-half miles into the air. The eastern mountains eclipsed the early sun, delaying mornings by a couple hours, but in the evening, the sun splashed into the deep after spreading its fire across the water's surface and shining its pink glow against the Gracens.

As the rays filtered through his surrounding forest, Makail blinked his eyes for the first time that day. Letting out a deep breath, he staggered to his feet, losing his balance slightly, before settling his hand on a tree to keep from falling. His restless night made him more wary than usual, for he normally roused long before the sun beamed down on his dwelling. But he couldn't sleep last night; his mind continued to wander to the journey of tomorrow. Tomorrow had neared more quickly than he had ever imagined, despite spending his past thirteen years preparing for the day. The day he would escape entirely from Dymetrice.

He peered east in the direction of King Avar's castle. In a small village, not a mile from the castle, Makail had once lived with his parents. As his searching eyes filled with shrubbery and mountain walls, he recalled the final day he beheld his parents. Just a child of eleven years, his parents spoke to him like a man. The words resounded through his head every day since. He holds vivid memories of the conversation that day.

"Makail, my son, you are blessed with the gifts of your mother and myself. The gifts this king believes we'd use against him. The gifts that have forced our king to end our lives." Makail remembers the flutter in his father's voice that day, for his father knew within hours, his life—and his wife's life—would be taken. The conversation he had that day was also the first time he recalls his parents talking at length of the gods and the gifts they'd bestowed upon them. "But son, you must not let this happen to you. Go to the mountains rising over the western woods, befriend the animals, but most importantly, master your gifts, son, master your gifts. As Omnerce, the God of Gods, endowed me, you can run faster and jump farther than anyone could fathom; as Alteight, the Goddess of Elevation, provided me, you can scale the steepest cliffs with swift ease; as Gusteeze, the Goddess of Wind, granted me, you can bounce people hundreds of yards with a gentle shove; and as Crusattle, the God of War, chose me, you can become the greatest swordsman who ever lived."

His mom intervened, "You will set fires with a wave of your hand, like Blazame, the God of Fire, blessed to me; you will make mountains crumble before you, as Rubbeak, the God of Mountains, granted me; you will cause enormous waves to crash against the shores, as Watea, the Goddess of the Deeps, gifted me; and you will tip trees with a flick of your finger, as Forber, the Goddess of Trees, set upon me. You will become the storm. Nothing will be greater than your capabilities."

"You will be the most extraordinary man to ever live." His father continued. "And for your mother and me to sacrifice our own lives to keep you safe, it is more than worth it. Our gifts have combined, and over time, will multiply within you. These gifts were granted to your mother and me to help our former queen, daughter of Omnerce, keep her mass brilliant. And now, your powers will far exceed our own, but you cannot let King Avar find you, for he will be rid of you because you are the offspring of us—the most untrustworthy residents of his land, in his eyes. He will do to you what looms for us. And that cannot happen, as your powers can save Prodigion from this Dymetrice king."

Makail sat attentively, facing his parents, absorbing everything. And his mother carried on, "My sweet child, it is an immense order what we ask of you, but the purpose of our union was you. You meant everything to us long before your birth, which is why we fled our former mass, an attempt to reach and sustain peace throughout the masses. Your safety is of utter importance to us, and we will no longer be here to protect you. You must protect yourself. The western forest is the safest place for you to hone your gifts. Then, my son," she glanced to her husband then back to Makail, "you will leave Dymetrice." She paused, imagining the difficulty of leaving his motherland, but she knew it would be what her son had to do. "You will leap over Threatle Gap and continue southwest through the gates of Pithlyn. In

Pithlyn, you will find Bidellia, and you will choose your steps, but she will keep you safe for all of time."

For the first time since his father began speaking, Makail, opened his mouth, "Who's Bidellia?" he asked with his eyes bouncing from each parent.

"You will discover this in time," his father replied. "Now, though, you must go. The king's men will be here in no time, and we are at our end. When you reach your destination, you can hunt and fish, as we've done together; you can heat your dinner by setting small fires as your mother has always done for us. You will take these: My sword with which you will train; my cloak for warmth on cool nights; these clothes of mine, which you will grow into; your mother's and my silver bracelets, which symbolize our eternal unity," genuinely glancing to his wife, "eternal bliss; a canteen for your thirst; and this bag. You will walk through this town casually, friendly to those who acknowledge you, but do not ask for help or converse extensively. Once you've reached the prairie, continue north to avoid another small village northwest of us. After you have traveled far enough north, head west until the Dymetrice River. This river is the trail to your new home, and you will see the mountains of Quintix Valley long before you reach them."

As he said "new home," Makail sat, panged with the

Chapter 1

sorrow of never seeing his parents again, never showing them what he learned today, never asking them of childhood mysteries, never telling them how much he loves them for everything. He only had them for eleven years and then it was goodbye forever. Why would King Avar take away a child's most important lifelines? "You two can't leave me!" Makail remarked, scared. "I need you—you have to be here for me. Run away with me!"

In a bold voice, his father injected, "We cannot run with you, Makail. The king's men would search high and low for us. But more importantly, our number has been called, and we cannot flee from our own death. Others believe, the powers of your mother and myself are not supposed to be inherited, but you possess them! They will never suspect you to have such inconceivable skills. We must sacrifice our own life so that you may live to see your own potential reach its pinnacle."

"Our unified blood runs through you; our flesh envelops you; we move with your every motion; and we are always within you. You see, we will always be with you," his mother comforted. "You will always speak to us, and we will always listen. We love you more than anything on this sphere, and you will always know this. Never forget our love. Carry it close to you through all your travels."

Makail's father continued, motioning toward himself,

The Storm

"Come, son. Let us have this final embrace, and then we will part. We love you son." The three of them tucked close together within each other, weeping. "I love you mother. I love you father."

After moments, "Now, son, you must go. Never forget our love. It will carry you through everything," his father ended. Makail stepped away from the hut of his parents.

The journey ahead of him that day resembled much of the journey ahead of him now: an unfamiliar destination, alone to discover meaning, and again, a new way of life. With the imminent expedition, however, Makail was ready. In his youth, he could not have prepared himself for the voyage his parents abruptly placed in front of him. However, if that journey had not been in his wake, he would never have developed into the man he'd become, the man prepared to reach the gates of Pithlyn and find safety under Bidellia then avenge the deaths of his parents.

Quintix Valley

To prepare for the day ahead of him, Makail heeded the words of his parents throughout his adolescence and into early adulthood. After days of mourning the overwhelming loss of his parents, he quickly began toiling with the gifts bestowed upon him. His parents had conferred every grain of knowledge they had to offer, so his first ten years of life were spent learning everything he could. His parents prepared him to be on his own; his parents knew King Avar would not let such potential betrayal continue to threaten his reign. Many knew the past of Makail's parents, so Isnelle and Jivin became King Avar's first target under his new order. However, not a soul outside their hut knew of Makail's potential. He acted and sounded like a normal child when relating with others. Jivin only allowed his son to practice his arts when nobody scattered the land within miles, which only occurred when Makail's father carried him on his back, whistling through the wind, to find a quiet region. Makail learned from his father how to run, jump, hunt, use a sword, and from his mother, he learned how to interact with people, show love, express kindness. Makail, in his first days without his parents, felt like he had so much more to learn about his own life, but he would soon discover the only learning he had left must be realized on his own.

When he first arrived to Quintix Valley, the scarcity of animals caused him to worry. As days continued to pass, he noticed he would never grow hungry. Even though there may have been few animals compared to other popular regions of Dymetrice, plenty existed to last one person more than a lifetime. A couple dozen grilk inhabited the two-hundred-mile expanse of wilderness, and all of them had spawn, shummies, who were very loyal to mom—without mom, they're lost. The husky grilks had narrow faces compared to their thick, bushy necks. They had massive bodies and each of their four legs carried as much girth as Makail's young waist. An average grilk weighed eight hundred pounds. The most unique part of the grilk was the horns emerging from their heads. The horns grew upward, sometimes three feet long with smaller spikes poking out, like thorns on a rose stem, only bigger. Longer horns meant more meat.

Chapter 2

For food supply purposes, one grilk would allow Makail to eat for a year, as long as he kept the meat shaded and away from other animals. He accomplished this by burying his food, knowing he could clean it in the stream, and cook away any other potentially harmful substances the ground may hold for it. Noticing a spoiled appearance and flavor after too long, he decided to store it atop the mountains in snowcapped regions.

In addition to the grilks, this forest inhabited eskeys, coyogs, capisongs, turnobings, and faselots. The eskeys were playful animals who loved climbing and jumping trees with their limber bodies. Makail found several eskeys to become good friends with him. They had pale faces perfectly encircled by thin, puffy hair; they could walk on two feet, but when one need to hurry, it would scuttle on all fours. The coyogs also found friendship in Makail. The four-legged coyogs had shapely bodies as a sign of good health; their tail wagged two feet long, and their heads were proportionately small with eyes above long snouts, which end with their nose and mouth. The long snouts make for deep mouths full of strong sharp teeth, which, combined with a superior sense of smell, help them hunt.

Two families of capisongs occupied the eastern corner of the valley where the mountains turned. Makail enjoyed visiting these extraordinary animals simply to survey their actions and remain in awe of such a creature. The capisongs had red fur and gray stripes on the upper portion of all four legs. When standing, their shoulders set five feet above the ground, and a four-foot neck separated the shoulders from the head. The head still had the same red fur with gray marks on either side. Atop the head, two small knobs pointed to the sky between droopy red ears. Their sticky gray tongues allowed for easier feeding, as they ate leaves and other plants. This animal's greatest talent, however, was their humming. The adult capisongs would hum a low-pitched, wavy melody to the younger ones in an effort to get them to sleep. The tune would begin soft then boom, alternating with inhales and exhales from the adult. The pure sound portrayed divine music. Makail practiced mimicking the tone of such a basic lullaby, and it became his favorite way of falling asleep.

Other than fish and grilk, Makail hunted the turnobings and faselots. Turnobings were most recognizable by their long, muscular tails. Their black-furred bellies and four legs looked too fat to fit the face, which resemble that of a coyog, only stouter. Two stiff white whiskers poked out on each side of the brown face behind its black nose. The strength of these animals caused them to carry excessive weight, though reducing their speed during a hunt. With this lack of speed, they either ate berries—especially the dark, sweet bing cherries—or they turn their face in the opposite direction of their prey, with hopes of being unnoticed, and smack the lesser animal with that bulky tail to stun it. On the contrary, the faselot hunted by catching its prey, as they ran faster than any other animal in Quintix Valley. Such speed was necessary for these animals since their bright yellow hair glittered with black specks caused them to stand out in the caliginous woods. A typical hunter of the faselot needed to possess quick reflexes and enough speed not to lose one, but Makail managed to exceed their pace.

Smaller animals also existed. Scaly creatures settled in the woods closer to the water and smaller, rodent-like animals could be found anywhere farther from the shoreline. The smallest of animals, bugs, from little to big, crept throughout the entire valley. Birds built nests in a variety of trees, but causing peaks along mountainsides, the largest birds, gantors, constructed dwellings large enough to hold Makail.

Nonetheless, Makail had built his own dwelling. By the end of his first twenty days alone, he had found the perfect location to create an adequate shelter for himself. He had grown wary of sleeping with critters under his father's cloak, covering his face and all on the rainy nights. Some nights had rainfalls lasting far into the next day, but he didn't mind the wet as long as he could persist with his daily efforts. Regardless, he knew the nights would better benefit him if he could build something to shield him. Knowing he wanted a home overlooking the water, he found the perfect spot not far above the base of the mountain closest to the ocean in the southern region of Quintix Valley. He knew he wanted his home to oversee the water. Envisioning his desires, he held up his fist; opening his palm, he began to slowly lower his arm. When he opened his eyes, a small portion of the mountain fizzled into pebbles, spilling to the ground below. The act carved out three walls and a floor. The back wall spanned nearly twenty-five feet with a height three times his own eleven-year stature.

Building the roof and front wall turned out more difficult than he'd expected. He built these barriers from the timber tipped by his fingertips, and he separated trunks of trees from the numerous branches by touching his fingertip where he wanted it to break, just like tipping an entire tree, leaving him with what he needed. His friendly eskeys helped haul the trunks to the new home. Using his sword, he carved a right angle to fit against the mountain. He also made sure to tip enough smaller trees so he could build an eight-foot tall opening on the front, giving him a door. Constructing the roof, which he did after completion of the front wall, provided the highest level of difficulty, knowing he'd need to angle it down from the mountain to his front wall. Fortunately, the eskeys possessed excellent climbing skills like him. But the difficulty came in fastening each log to the previous at the same angle. To fasten the wood, he retrieved enough sea ribbons from the shallow waters. The inch-wide sea ribbons flexibility called for weakness, but if someone tried to pull one in half, the durable plant could resist all forces. When a sea ribbon dried, it locked in its position nearly unbreakable. Makail weaved the sea ribbon through the wood along the sides, binding each log together. Due to the naturally varying shape of each log, small spaces occurred in areas. To resolve this issue, Makail dug under the thin layer of sand not deep into the water where he found a tough, mushy material. After sealing the gaps, he'd completed his house where he would sleep joined by his eskey and coyog friends.

Hunting and fishing came naturally to him. His father had superior tactics, which he shared with his son. The first forty days in the valley, Makail had stuck with fishing while practicing sword maneuvers through the air. The sword practice, he intended, would come in handy when hunting his first larger animal. But in his first many days, he'd had to fish because he had to eat, and he understood how to prepare a fish after catching one since he attentively observed his father clean a fish with the same sword Makail would now use. The first fish he reeled in caught him by surprise, as he did not expect a surplus of fish near the shore. Therefore, he excitedly began the cleaning phase of fishing. When he was ready to cook it, he gathered several twigs that had fallen from the trees, constructed a small pile; then he opened his palm, closed his eyes, envisioned a small flame, and then he opened his eyes to the burning twigs. He stuck the fish meat on his sword, watching it sizzle up to the perfect temperature.

Eventually, he began using his sword to hunt the grilks, turnobings, and faselots. The handle of his sword came up to his chest while the point jabbed the ground. This handle shined. Where the blade and handle met, gold seeped to each side finishing with a curl both upward and downward. The large handle, which extended longer than his young forearm, had half-inch glistening pebbles in a line down the front and back, each pebble a different color. He used this sword proudly, feeling like he could take on the world with it in his hand, even though it remained too large for him until he neared his full growth around the age of seventeen, which was also when his father's cloak began to fit him like a warrior.

He exercised with his sword every day in Quintix Valley. With imaginary enemies, he rehearsed the lessons his father had passed to him. Quickly mastering those tactics, he moved to designing his own maneuvers, working on a quick draw of the sword to block an unexpected attack; jabbing to his right and left fast enough to appear in one motion; adding small, dodging jumps and powerful kicks to make sure he could fight with foot and sword at once; improving to collaborate combination moves with low kick, high kick, sword swipe; never fatiguing. He even made himself proficient as a left-handed puncher despite the better coordination on his right side, but the right hand always holds the sword. His sword became fast and powerful, and his muscles grew distinctly throughout his arms, chest, and stomach as a result of his relentless training.

When he could set the sword aside, Makail ran. The lightning speed he possessed the first time he set foot in Quintix Valley only progressed. He zipped along the grassy expanse just beyond the shoreline on a daily basis, making it from the valley's edge to the opposite border and back within an hour, never fatigued. Impossibly fast. He also bolted to the summits of mountains without taking a break between climbs. He shivered in stride when the oxygen became scant and temperatures below freezing, but he never lingered in those regions more than a minute. The cliffs on some of the mountains slowed him down from time to time, but he learned to effortlessly scale the steepest walls without ever feeling fatigue.

In addition to setting fires for cooking he made bigger fires with plants standing closer to mountains' bases, not disturbing the homes of various animals. When he produced a fire, there was never a flaring streak of flames lashing toward his fire point; rather, he'd visualize where he wanted the fire to erupt, then like magic, the fire would burn. Creating fires allowed for two things: warmth on a cool night and practice. He worked on configuring larger flames with the shrubbery, learning to harness his fire.

At night, he'd often sit in his doorway, watching the soft roll of the gray waves steadily trickle into the shore. With the moonlight shining on the water's surface, he marveled at such a spectacle, before wishing the waves to enlarge with white crests spiraling to the sand. Thus, he'd close his eyes, spreading his arms, keeping his palms up, while softly flapping his hands and picturing the waves he wanted. He'd open his eyes and watch the froth-tipped waves explode on the sand.

For all the years he spent in Quintix Valley, he never wasted a moment. Constantly, he worked on improving his skills. His parents had made it very clear to him that he has important and remarkable gifts. Makail knew his parents would have never wanted to see him waste the glory of gods' blessings. Makail had also figured out why he possesses such great power. His parents had wanted him to come to Quintix Valley to hone his gifts, become the most remarkable man ever to live, and travel to Pithlyn to meet a lady named Bidellia. What was never spoken, however, held the most pertinent idea of their entire stratagem. He had to conquer King Avar and all of Dymetrice.

His rigorous training revealed his strong desire to fulfill his parents' dying wish. Nine days prior to the day he would leave Quintix Valley, he had one final act to ensure his gifts could not be improved upon, to ensure he'd perfected his gifts. His practice in Quintix Valley proved evident in all of his skills, especially his swordsmanship. He could stir his sturdy sword better than anyone, and he looked forward to proving it.

On that ninth day before departing, he trekked toward the center of the valley where he stabbed his sword a quarter deep. Content, he made his way to the shoreline. He found several eskeys and coyogs, even a few turnobings, and escorted them to a point in the woods beyond his sword. The turnobings, though, did not cooperate as well, so Makail helped them out with a gentle shove, flinging them through the trees. Finally reaching the shore, he stood facing all the trees of the valley bordered by the mountains. He admired his home of thirteen years, recalling all the time he spent with the animals, with himself. He considered how far he had come and how this area allowed for him to grow from a boy to a man.

He came back to the present time, knowing he had an order of business to conduct. With his eyes open, he floated his open palm across the front row of trees, blazing every one of them to a wondrous fire. The leaves crackled and the wood popped within the orange, blending to red flames. The smoke rose high into the dusky torch-lit sky. Makail admired his work briefly then tilted his head back and stretched his arms wide with his palms up, slowly bringing his hands up. As his hands neared each other, he clinched them to a fist, swiping them down to his sides. When his hands hit his hips, the massive half-mile-high tidal wave he'd created gulped ten miles of Quintix Valley's western front. When his hands hit his hips, he dashed, leaping over his flames. The leap carried him all the way to his sword, where he flipped his head toward the ground; plunging his arms over his head, he grasped his sword and came to a rolling halt. He propelled his sword so fast it looked like a glistening silver-filled circle, before slapping it into its case. Raising his fists outward, he opened his palms and delicately sunk them toward his waist, and he watched the boulders of mountain mass tumble before that first row of trees, allowing water to seep back to the ocean, while blocking the destroyed trees from entering the sea.

The following several days, Makail mended the destruction of his storm. He rolled trees to fittingly embed them about the open expanse his wave caused. He proudly picked up the western portion of Quintix Valley, as he knew his powers exceeded that of his parents' dreams. He knew he had become the most extraordinary man in the world. With that notion, he was ready to embark on his next journey.

Dymetrice Wall

Makail readied himself for the journey ahead. He grabbed his hair, which draped halfway down his back, pulled it in front of him, and hacked it, making it higher than shoulder length. With his blade he gently skimmed along his face, removing thick facial hair. He put on his father's thin black pants and black shirt, which had sleeves hardly covering his shoulders. The cloak he'd once used as a sheet for warmth slung from his shoulders to the back of his knees. Barefoot, he walked toward the water, considering the day ahead. As he reached the water, he peered down to see his reflection. Though he'd shaven himself well, he held a rugged appearance. He had a sharp jaw bone, leading up to indented temples. His full lips rested calm under his modest nose. His eyes beat dark brown, matching his hair and the wet sand beneath his feet. His thick, muscular neck led into his broad shoulder, which grew into brawny arms. And his robust chest thumped with the courage of a warrior. Yes, he was ready.

Before he could leave Quintix Valley, he ran to his home to meet with his closest eskeys and coyogs. "This is the day my friends. Today is the reason I came to this valley. Today," and each of the dozen animals within his home stared at the man speaking in front of them, "I will begin the voyage my parents lined up for me before I came here. You have all been wonderful company for me, and my stay here in Quintix Valley would have been dreadful without you. You are all my friends, and I will never forget the meals we shared and the comfort we brought to each other. I hope you will all continue on to lead healthy and strong lives. I will miss each and every one of you, and I will never forget any of you." He continued through each of the animals, petting them individually, and kissing the coyogs on the tops of their heads. The eskeys, on the other hand, opened their arms to give him a farewell hug. As he walked away, Makail could hear eskey chirps behind him, as if they were cheering him on to have a successful adventure.

Once he'd completely passed the mountain, he ran through the rest of the forest, halting when he drew next to the final row of trees. Makail stepped into the sunlight. For the first time since his trek to Quintix

Valley years ago, he saw green pastures before him. His mouth slightly open, he took in the simplest view, as if it were a wonder to behold. He gaped back to the valley where the high eastern sun bounced off the mountains and set a hazy glow across the treetops. The gray clouds of the westerly sky contrasted starkly with the east's blue satin. The green grass in front of him absorbed the sun, and walking through it, he felt free.

His pace remained steady, for he was unfamiliar with the surroundings, even though he didn't stray far from water to his right. He had no idea if the next village lay one mile away or one hundred miles. Numerous trails wore in the grass from people walking to the sea for a supply of water, so he knew a good possibility existed of passing a man or woman walking on one of the paths. Thus, he could not run like the blazes where people would spot him. Makail had to be normal. The inherited gifts killed his parents, and the same could never hold true for him.

After walking long enough for the distant gray clouds and the sun to converge, he came to a village. Many huts lined dirt trails, and he could see children playing and mothers watching over them. He watched the children smacking wooden swords against, one another while smiling, happy. The mother's looked on laughing and talking amongst themselves. One of the mothers peaked her head toward Makail, but Makail hadn't noticed, as he kept his eyes on the wooden sword fight, playful training of youth.

"Are you lost, young man," her voice called out.

Whipping his attention toward the huddle of women, he felt out of place. "No, ma'am."

She continued walking toward him, "You need not call me ma'am. We must be near in age. My child's friends will call me ma'am, but not a lost man."

"I am not lost, lady. I just saw the young sword fight and became entertained for a moment."

"It's Wava," she warned.

"I'm sorry?"

"My name is Wava, not ma'am, not lady, Wava."

"Makail," he responded, as she had made it within arm's reach of him. Her green eyes squinted in the sun. Her brown hair breezed with the slight wind, and she had soft facial features. A delicate woman, standing only as tall as Makail's chest. "But I'll continue on my way now. It was nice to meet you."

"What is your destination?" her thin lips asked.

He hesitated, knowing he couldn't answer honestly. "Dymetrice Point, and I will fish."

"Nobody makes it to Dymetrice Point, not since the raising of the Dymetrice Wall. You can fish anywhere, why would you want to go to a place where you'll be cut off by the guards?"

"Stranger, I do not wish to share my intentions with somebody I just met."

"Then tell me this," she challenged. "From where do you meander with this sword and cloak? The sphere is silent, at peace; there is no battle here."

"The sword is for my hunt, and the cloak is for the imminent rain. My travels today began from Quintix Valley." he said simply.

"Hunting in Quintix Valley… no wonder your hands are empty." Then her eyes grew skeptical. "What is it you hunt, if you are not traveling to fish?"

She almost caught him in the lie, but he had a sly response, avoiding her trap "I will hunt the fish with my sword."

"Ha, no man stabs a fish in water with his sword, especially without bait."

"I correct you, Wava." He stepped closer, growing intense with annoyance. "No man you had ever met hunts fish solely with sword, until you met me. I'll be on my way before the man who wears your matching bracelet discovers you talking with a stranger."

"Nonsense. He has no worry, for I am his, and everybody knows it. He will not grow jealous. And you should not speak to a woman as if her intentions are foul."

Chapter 3

"My apologies ma'—Wava."

"Before you pass this commune, why is it you wear two bracelets? Have you lost your love?"

Makail looked to both his wrists, and his throat constricted. He'd never spoken to another human about it. "They are my parents'. They were killed in my youth. Wearing these bracelets gives me another way to remember them." He turned southwest, away from Wava and her village. He looked back one final time, catching her soft green eyes. "Silence is always the predecessor of chaos."

His journey continued as light raindrops began to slip from the sky. He took his left hand, grabbing the bottom of his cloak and throwing it over his right shoulder. He kept his arms folded under the cloak to stay warm in the cool rain. The ground below him remained his only view for much of the march, only peering up on a few occasions to see his surroundings. He never crossed another village before he caught sight of Dymetrice Wall. As the sun pursued westerly horizons, the wall shined in the hazy air. It had been built from the rarest of granites. The smooth, bleak sides produced seamless streaks of trickling rain. The top rose thirty feet from the ground with sporadic concavely curved points, adding another eight feet. He considered jumping over it, but thinking better of it, there might be a doorway to pass through. He followed the wall from north bearing south, remaining a couple miles from the wall. He continued to view south from where he trekked when he noticed the glossy black arching upward. The arch began like the occasional points had, but instead of coming back to the surface, it continued toward the sky. That had to signify his opening. Excited, Makail began walking faster, turning his stride into a soft run, and he could see the passageway to Dymetrice Point. The opening had a flat ceiling with the solid arch above it, and a spread of about ten feet. He could see through the entryway, and he headed toward it. Within a mile of the wall, he stopped.

A gargentwan stood each side of the doorway. Their stature took up two-thirds the height of the wall. Makail had never seen such a being, but from his childhood he could recall his parents describing the gargentwans of northern Glaci. These two men, more than twice as tall as the capisongs he'd visited in Quintix Valley, had heavily robust chest and even broader shoulders with arms of more girth than Makail's chest. Their legs held the circumference of a tree trunk and the strength of a freight train. Flesh and face, however, appeared human. Despite the proportional size of their heads, the features of their face were exactly like that of any other man walking the sphere.

Through the thickening rainfall and gashing lightning,

Makail could see they wore nothing above their waist and had similar thin black pants to what Makail was wearing. Unlike Makail's, their pants had a black belt lining the waist, holding additional weaponry. Each of their hands held thick steel rods that ended with a steel ball ringed with a blade.

Not deterred, Makail crept closer. Both sets of gargentwan eyes pierced down on him, as he continued toward them. He thought perhaps he could just walk right through without acknowledging either of them. He'll mind his business, and they'll mind theirs? Unfortunately for Makail, their business was the passageway. As he came within five strides of the opening, both steel spheres slammed into the ground crossing each other to form an X. "Where do you think you are going?" said a thunderous voice, like boulders collapsing from a mountain.

"Pithlyn."

"Ha, you will never cross to Pithlyn. This is our land. You will remain in Dymetrice," boomed the one to Makail's left, Junder.

Makail back pedaled a few strides. Ignoring the words of the gargentwan, he stared at the two of them, noting their immensity, and asked, "King Avar doesn't trust anybody outside of Dymetrice, so how is it the two of you are allowed to pull duty guarding his gates?"

The one to Makail's right spoke in the same rough tone. "We heard of the gate several years ago. Our leaders name is Hilbran. He requested to watch this wall. We promised never to allow an exit for one who may carry deep Dymetrice secrets. We promised never to allow entry to unwanted foes. Hilbran discussed this with King Avar. He discussed our wishes with Pithlyn's queen. The queen agreed since it would provide a secure line from Dymetrice entry. King Avar agreed after we promised loyal duty or death. We rotate guards every two years. Two more of our men come down to replace. That is when our duty is complete."

Makail swallowed the unexpected in-depth description and pressed, "Why did you want to leave your homeland?"

Most people who passed by the guards never spoke to them. Everybody feared their appearance, so Makail's questions allowed the two to open up as they never had, even though the purpose of Makail's questions pried for weaknesses, knowing he must elude them and get through the wall to Pithlyn.

"We left to spread gargentwan need throughout the sphere," Tyban responded. "This was the first step in allowing us to mix our kind with all else."

"But you guys are huge. How could you possibly mix in anywhere?" he continued with a sly smirk.

Chapter 3

"Do not judge us!" Junder roared, picking up his staff and crashing it at Makail's feet.

Makail skipped back to avoid contact. "I'm not saying you're fat or anything. With your size," he considered his words carefully, attempting to compliment, "each of you could take on five guys at once. It must be incredible to be so powerful."

"We are powerful," Tyban said. "We could swipe you into the without even making an effort."

"Ah, that won't be necessary. I'll just travel on to Pithlyn, and you two can relax and wait for the next person who comes by."

"Scoundrel will not leave Dymetrice!"

"Why not?"

"You will never get by us. We are powerful."

"And a bit maxed out on yourselves."

The gargentwans stood ten feet apart from each other. With rain continuing to spurt down on them and distant lightning followed by the soft gurgle of thunder, Makail sized them up. Before, either had an opportunity to react, Makail had leaped toward Tyban only to spring off his thigh, thrust his feet into Junder's chest, bouncing him away and propelling himself toward Tyban. Flying over Tyban's right shoulder, he latched onto it with his right hand, swinging himself chest to back on his foe. Makail began to slide down when he shoved the gargentwan from behind, catapulting him through the air. Makail landed and saw Tyban land right on top of Junder. Assessing the downed gargentwans, Tyban brought himself to foot, drawing his sword. He turned with eyes full of aggravation; Junder scampered to follow, mimicking Tyban's every motion. Makail clutched his sword as the gargentwans began charging for him. They both had their steel sphere and a sword in hands. Makail waited as the two enclosed him, attacking. The gargentwans thrashed their blades on him, and he blocked everything with his quick sword. Two blades came at him simultaneously and repeatedly. Two after two from over his head, smashing down to his sword.

Knowing their focus solely rested on defeating him, Makail continued to block the onslaught with furious twitches, while backtracking through the wall's opening. Once through, he turned his back pedal south. The enraged assault never let up. Just before Makail was ready to make his move, Tyban slashed high with his sword while striking Makail on the side with the steel rod, overextending the bladed sphere. The force of the shaft drove him aside, and he perched on the ground. He looked to the south; he could see where Dymetrice Point fell off to the cliff reaching the sea—not too far away. He rose to his feet, winced briefly, then sped toward the one who'd struck him. He jumped over the brute, landing behind him and whirling with his arms cocked. Plunging his arms into the back, he flung Tyban over the edge to splash in the Carné Sea. As Junder stood dumbfounded, Makail lunged toward his shoulders, grabbing a hold of his bare trapezoids with feet braced on that heavy chest. He flipped himself backward, spinning the creature with him. Once the gargentwan's back had rotated around to point toward the cliff, Makail pressed his legs against the chest, hurling him to meet his partner while Makail finished the rotation to land on his feet. He turned to face the stormy sea when his wave set in motion toward the two fiends, which carried the gargentwans to the cliff's incline, before sucking them under and bursting them into the sea until they individually realized they could bolster themselves to the sea floor and allow the rushing water to surge past them, leaving them to flounder alone in steady rain-drizzled water.

Makail brushed his hands together, thinking aloud, "Now who will guard the gate?" He lifted the right side of his shirt where contact had been made. The pinkish tone of his sore extended from the top of his hip to just beneath his chest. He rubbed it gingerly, praying the pain would soon be gone, for his remaining journey required godly efforts.

Pitblyn's Gates

"For far too many years, I've been alone, without a man to love and comfort me, and as I've sat upon the highest throne, I've never loved. Now think, how could this be?" Bidellia spoke in the day's late hour to her trusted noble advisor, Fidelis, from her soft, deep sapphire blue fleeced chair, which had solid gold trimming and matching armrests. Her chair sat on a platform eight steps above the floor yet beneath to massive forearms of gold, ending with open palms toward the sky—the hands of Omnerce. A sapphire carpet striped the center of the floor from the foot of her chair to the tall doors granting entry to the room. The morning sun shone through, leaving stretched windows glowing along the floor.

Her castle sprung in the deep divot of a double-peaked mountain. The front wall extended from the north mountain incline to the south mountain incline, using the mountains' surface as castle walls. Castle workers had applied a viscous tar to seal castle walls from the nature of rain and critters. This front wall, however, held much more width than the throne room, which kissed the southern mountain, but in the castle, five doors led from the throne room to other wings. Directly north, the door fed into a corridor with the head guards room first followed by Fidelis's room, and Queen Bidellia occupied the northernmost room, which had a rocky wall inside and a spaciously arching balcony outside. Moving one flip west, the door led to a room with twenty or so long, narrow tables, used as a dining hall and a full-castle meeting room. Behind the dining hall, a meal preparation room rested with plenty of creative meal designers working. The north door behind Queen Bidellia's throne opened to stairways. To the right, stairs descended to a base for a hairpin continuation to the castle's confinary, where illmates who'd wronged at the highest level were trapped. Straight ahead, stairs increased to a crossing hallway with guards rooms on both sides. Guards on the first level lived alone and fought in battle when necessary. Upwards stairs continued after the first hallway to a second level where single committee members dwelled in more spacious rooms equipped with desks and tables. The final flight of stairs ended on the final level of rooms, which consisted of a mix between guards and committee members. These rooms provided the most space for each individual inhabiting them because these individuals carried families, wife and child. The immediate southern door behind Queen Bidellia's throne gave way to a dazzling ball room. Once entering this room, the walls on the right and left made seven arched openings until the end of the room with four feet of wall separating each opening. Behind these arched openings lain a wood-paneled hallway with cushioned chairs lining the walls. On the four feet of wall hung golden framed artwork of nature, stars, and gods. Between the walls, a glossy nacreous floor bordered with that deep blue of the queen's chair gleamed beneath three golden, triple-ringed chandeliers suspended from the ceiling. At the opposite end of the room, a platform raised four steps above the floor fuzzed with Pithlyn blue. Behind the southernmost door, almost to the corner of the throne room hid the training room, which tailed into a swordsmithing region. Many guards and committee members worked hard to perfect their fighting ability, preparing if controversy ever shook. For the queen to admit one on her esteemed committee, one must have proven ability with a sword, and the guards must possess strength and swiftness.

Fidelis, a slimly built man with dark softly waving

hair, beady brown eyes, a narrow face covered with thin black hairs, and a nose slightly too large for his features, responded to her remarks, "My Queen, you have ruled our land with an unmatched passion. You have spread your love to all of those who occupy the Pithlyn soil. You rule your kingdom with generosity and fervor. The duties you hold as queen give you no time and no space within your chest to love a single man. And with all my respect, my Queen, no man of Pithlyn would ever be bold enough to believe he is worthy of your grace." As was his job, Fidelis answered honestly and with his Queen's best interest at heart. He never thought twice about what to say. She expected him to speak truth and wisdom.

She considered his words at length before responding. "It's true, my love is vast for all the men, the women, and the children of our land, yet men won't dare to share my love." She pondered her rule. Had she been too harsh of a leader? She had always been kind to those who fought for righteousness beside her. She always respected a man willing to die an admirable death for Pithlyn to breathe a deeper breath. She made herself approachable to all occupants of her land. She continuously showed her love to all.

"It is these men who view you as their beloved master, their Goddess" Fidelis began. "They will remain reverent before you. Never would they dream an interest from you beyond duty." Without realizing it, Fidelis began to convince her of something.

"So then," Bidellia continued, "if Pithlyn holds no man to grasp my hand, I'll search afar," she hesitated for a moment and stared at Fidelis, "but first, where shall I turn?"

"If you wish to search beyond Pithlyn ground to find a man whom you may believe to be worthy, your search is then but north, south, east, or west. For me to tell you which way to begin would be of hasty drivel, and I know you are not one to stand for that," he responded, baffled.

The queen kept an inquisitive glare on Fidelis. He typically had the answers for her, or at least demonstrated his support on a decision she'd made. As Fidelis remained blank in return to Bidellia, she began to decipher aloud which mass ought to hold the one for her. "Indiffrin, Zyder, Glaci, not a chance! Dymetrice, as a whole, I'd rather burn, but Favally just might be worth a glance."

Fidelis released a smirk, and Bidellia returned it with a wider smile. "You see," he started, "your wits will work through any quandary. We shall travel across the Pithlyn Pass into Favally to find your love. Let us rest now, for it is getting late."

Content, he turned to his right, beginning to walk toward the northernmost door to find his room. Then he stopped in stride. Spinning back to the throne, he hesitated before asking, "What if Favally does not have a man who is right for you? What if Glaci, Dymetrice, Zyder, and Indiffrin have no man who's perfect for you? I cannot serve a sullen queen without becoming apathetic, hence affecting my duties."

Though Fidelis had raised his tone by a level, she remained calm, and answered, "In all the land, there must be one with whom I'd share this life forever set to bloom."

"I hope you're right, my Queen." And Fidelis left her at peace to dwell within her own ideas.

After disassembling the guards, Makail soon realized he hadn't eaten since morning. The cliff near him dropped two hundred feet to the sea with a small landing area for the continuous gentle sloshes of natural waves. Walking to the southern edge, the steep, rain-slickened angle reminded him of all the mountain scaling he'd performed in Quintix Valley. Wasting no time, he poised himself for the descent, and in no time, his feet dampened with the calm rush of waves. Rain dabbed the water's surface like pellets while lightening shredded the distant sky followed by a gentle bustle of thunder. He wondered how far out the undertow of his colossal wave had shot the two gargentwans. Siphoned through a gusting stream after the power of Makail's waves, the two may have drowned before their bodies came to the surface. On the other hand, considering the lung capacity of gargentwans, they likely survived a two-mile underwater tour of the Carné Sea.

A murky scene brought low vision for Makail, as he pursued his dinner. Although, when lightening flashed, he could see clearly through the water. He began timing the sporadic lightening, and once he'd advanced waist-deep, he could see a few fish within arm's reach. The next zap of lightening came with his simultaneous plunk; lifting his sword from the water, a large fish dangled and squirmed from his sword. On his sludge back to the narrow coast, lightening bolted again, and another fish right wiggled next to him, doubling his dinner. Arriving at the cliff's base, he prepared both fish, before starting a fire to cook them. He ate the two without stopping to catch his breath.

Makail, knowing the obscurity of night, and his lack of familiarity with Dymetrice Point, decided it would be safer to run the narrow trail before climbing up. Dymetrice Point, however, inclined all the way to Threatle Gap, causing a longer eventual climb. The most important thing to Makail was simply finding the gap, and he knew if he could zip across the base of the cliff, he'd assume no risk of someone seeing as opposed to running the grassy top of Dymetrice Point. Therefore, he dashed, focusing on his minute lane, keeping an eye on the cliff to his right because once the cliff no longer appeared, he'd be in the middle of the sea within seconds. His focus intensiveness him to stop on point once he reached the cliff's end where he immediately began his rise to the top, scaling the impossible, impossibly fast.

Atop the cliff, he gazed on the vast body of water below him. The rain had softened, and the low rumbles of thunder had quieted long after lightening flickered. A light breeze persisted, causing a constant sweeping of waves, leaving a wondrous, unsteady face. He marveled at the view; he loved the scene of water everywhere. Not a piece of land within sight, aside from that which rested beneath his feet. The land on which he stood had a curved edge, dwarfing to the drop. Dymetrice Point did not end with a sharp point but a rounded brink. Only six feet separated one side from the other, but it was still different from what Makail had expected. As the land continued east toward Dymetrice, it widened quickly, like a cone. Grass blanketed the land with trees sprouting throughout the expanse.

Despite the view halting him, Makail began to wonder how he will aim his jump since he had no clue of his landing mark. Should he jump and land in water to swim the rest of the way? Such a method would give him a precautionary measure in case a guard waited at the opposite tip. With a nod of his head, he answered his own thoughts. He turned away from the land's edge, scanning his surroundings for any nomads. He walked back half a mile from his jumping point. Feeling safe, he lined himself with the edge to jump straight from its center, following the provided angle. With an unruffled fury, he whipped through the grass and sprung into the air above Threatle Gap.

His legs continued to pump as if he ran on solid ground, but he fled through the air as fast as a shooting star. He wanted to peek down to see if he could find a large sea creature, like what his parents had described to him, but he maintained his focus. Any lapse of concentration would cause him to lose his leap, sending him downward with much more to swim than he preferred. He drove his arms, like a sprinter, keeping his head forward. He knew he'd already passed the apex of his bound, but he stretched for more distance. As the sea's surface became more and more near, he braced his strides for the impact, allowing his bare feet to swiftly graze the water—still running in stride—before reaching his ankles, knees, and hips. As his hips entered the water, he bent his torso to begin a swimming motion. He whooshed through the water, gradually slowing his pace so he could eventually flounder to view his whereabouts. Knowing he needed to keep his direction, his first sight bowed straight ahead. Through the clear dusky air, he could see the silhouette of a giant crag equal in height to where he'd jumped. He could not have been more than ten miles from the land, so he swam a steady tempo the rest of the way, reaching his immediate destination well before dawn.

Once he arrived at the tall rock formation, he sat at the base and looked out to sea. Much like on the other end of Threatle Gap, water filled his eyes in every direction. Soft waves dribbled to his feet. He hooked his head around to observe the narrow coastline before a cliff, quickly swiveling to view the other side. Had he some how become turned around during his leap? The cliff's base resembled exactly Dymetrice Point. In a state of anxiety, he jumped to grab hold of a crevice in the rocky wall, beginning his quick ascent. Gripping the peak, he hauled himself upward, landing on the grass. He walked a couple strides north and south, noting the same exact distance as from where he'd begun his leap. Furious, he walked hastily away from the tip. He stopped. Darkness still shaded every bit of land, but as he looked around, he discerned the differences in tree locations. He no longer stepped on the grounds of King Avar. This land belonged to Pithlyn, and he felt a rush of freedom.

Makail dashed along the northern edge. He could feel

the proximity of his aim. He felt as though he'd already entered the kingdom. He knew if he could get rid of two gargentwans, Pithlyn would have no such guard brave enough to fight him off or obstinate enough to stop him. He knew he was immediately bound to enter Pithlyn. His thoughts halted with his feet, as he looked onto a giant wall, shimmering with gold in the gloomy air. This wall was not quite as tall as the black one of Dymetrice, but just as sturdy. There were no curved points on this wall either. Instead, in the distance to the south of Makail, he could see two torches lit on miniature towers atop the wall. Other than the two cylinders, the walls top remained flat as far as it extended from north to south. Makail walked toward the flames.

Not quite making it to the flames, he saw nine men, walking in line circling the grounds before the doorway. These ordinary men stood no taller than Makail, each with a cased sword on their left leg. They wore white from the neck down with golden cloaks, waving behind them. The men marched in unison, evenly spaced until the last in line, for there a larger gap prevailed from the last in line to the first in line. The white top of the front guard had a gold stripe on each arm. Makail, who stood at a distance outside of earshot, assumed he was in charge of the squad. Therefore, he would time his encounter to meet the front guard first.

Chapter 4

Makail slowly crept closer. His all black attire allowed for cautious camouflage before sunup. Holding his green cloak tightly against his back concealed the slightest bit of unusual motion, potentially piquing the guards' attention. At a tree, a hundred yards in front of the wall, Makail hid in the branches. He looked in on the doorway straight in front of him, seeking the appropriate time to reveal himself. He observed the giant doors, as they appeared firmly sealed together. No lock existed, no handle either, just a slight cleft where the doors clapped. He noticed hinges along the sides, showing that the door can only be opened from the other side.

From his position in the tree, having timed the revolving men combined with knowing how quickly he'd reach their vision, he could make certain the leader would be the first to see him. Makail watched these guards circle a couple more times when the cleft of the door widened. From near the top of the wall, it slowly cracked open. And what appeared as a tiny figure next to the height of the door, a man, dressed like the other nine, peeked his head out, saying, "Alright men, almost dawn. Come in for a feed then we will switch." Seeing his opening, he thought quickly, and torched the tree from where he spied. As soon as he lit it aglow, he bolted south to another remote tree. From there, he watched the men charge toward the fire; all ten of them ran to check for danger, including the man who'd poked his head through the door. As Makail had envisioned, the door had had sprung open farther in the guards haste to reach the fire. As it steadily began to close, Makail ran as fast as lightening for it. Slipping through the creeping opening, he took one peak back to see the men waving their arms in an effort to put out the flames. Turning as the door shut behind him, he lowered his head, saying quietly, "Mom, Dad," he swallowed hard, praying they would hear him, "I'm in Pithlyn."

Kind Village

Large gold buildings, lined up evenly with the torches atop the wall, bordered his pathway. Just beyond the buildings' limits, a thin forest engulfed his vision. To avoid the sight of any lingering guards, Makail dashed to the forest, and climbed a tree a few rows deep. He stared back to the two buildings, realizing they held as homes for those who guard the door. The man who'd originally cracked the door open came back and screamed "Fire! Bring pails of water!" even louder, he repeated, "Fire!" Within seconds, throngs of men came rushing. A few had pails filled with water, others just ran to participate in the gawking. A few also remained close to the door, to protect the gates as many tended to the fire. From his tree, Makail could see the smoke writhing into the dawning sky. He remained calm in his place, recognizing these men's attention rested with the burning.

Kind Village

He remained in his position until the sun sparked over the golden wall, causing a blinding glisten. He turned away and dropped quietly from his tree. Walking through the forest with the pure scent of spring grass thrilling his senses, he felt alive and thriving yet weary of his grueling excursion. He wanted to fall on the forest's bed and rest, but he'd waited his entire life for this journey, so he had to press forth. He watched the ground under his slowly stepping feet through his dazey eyes. Taking a deep breath, he looked up at his surroundings, "So this is Pithlyn," he said to himself, "another forest."

Dawdling through the woods, the trees began to space apart more and more to where areas had entire aisles of treeless grass. On the southern horizon, visible form the open space, a mountain chain tickled the morning sky. To the north, land washed into water closing with the orange sky. Straight ahead, to the west, trees sporadically raised from the ground, yielding more of a prairie than a forest. Slightly south, Pithlyn's closest village to Dymetrice began to rouse. From Makail's distant sight, the huts appeared as anthills, yet he needed to make certain his sight retained a Pithlyn village. Gaping closer, he could see huts lining trails and decided on a whim, what he had to do.

With an exaggerated stagger, he closed in on the town. One man walked along a path, other than that, the town remained quiet. This man, Makail could see, had dark skin and stiffer, rounder hair that did not fall to the sides of his head. He was tall, not as tall as Makail, but taller than the average man. His arms developed a sturdy formation, and Makail could assume he worked a lot. As Makail approached, this Pithlyn man noticed him, and called out, "Young lad, have you lost your way?"

Makail returned nothing as he continued the act of a shattered stray. His wind drew heavy like a man hanging on for dear life. He arched his right side while keeping his left hand over it, signifying pain. The man he approached watched closely, and when Makail tried putting his right hand on the man's shoulder, the Pithlyn man bucked back, repeating "Are you lost?"

"Yes, I have lost my way," he confessed breathlessly.

"From where have you come to disturb my village at this early time?"

"I've run, and I fear I cannot run anymore," continuing his elongated breaths. "I am faint. I will break. I need your help."

He studied Makail for several moments. Feeling his pain and portrayed weakness, he said, "My name is Gonko." With a curious tone, he continued, "What kind of help do you seek?"

"Rest," he admitted still unable to catch his breath. "I've been battered and overly exerted. I cannot go on, kind Gonko."

"Battered? Is that why you hold your side there," he asked, gesturing toward Makail.

"Yes sir." Makail began to lift his shirt, revealing a deep red sore, which faded into a tone of purple toward the center, darkening at the point of contact. "It was a shaft, thick metal that could have gashed a hole in the mountain."

Gonko winced at the wound, before answering Makail's remark, "Your wound is obscene by nature, but if the shaft could damage a mountain, then why did it not splatter you through the air?"

"Yes, I'm sorry. I overstated the shaft's strength, but on impact, it felt as heavy."

"What is your name lad?"

"Makail," of Dymetrice, he wanted to add, but Gonko would have sent him along had he declared his mass of birth.

Notwithstanding, Gonko's second question: "Makail, what is your motherland?"

Grasping to catch his breath, "I am a Pithlyn man. My motherland is unknown, for I have been sent from one mass to the other all my life, but I will always claim Pithlyn as my motherland." The boldface lie of multiple degrees had to work, for he needed Gonko's help. Makail did not like lying to anybody, but he had no other choice under such circumstances.

"Then we both claim this land as our land. Therefore, you are my compé." A smile came to Gonko's face, as he went on, "The kush in my hut will remain empty for a great length from now. Please, Makail, use it for rest. When you wake, I will show you great healing."

"I am grateful for you, Gonko. May I ask one more favor of you?" As Gonko nodded his head, Makail continued, "Please do not wake me. Allow me to awaken naturally, for I have a long journey ahead of me. Can you do this for me? "

"Indeed. You shall rest. When you awake, naturally, you will tell me of your journey ahead."

Makail affirmed Gonko's statement with a head dip, before carrying through the village to the fourth hut on the right, which Gonko had pointed toward earlier as his. Makail looked back to Gonko, before entering the hut, to make sure this was the right dwelling for now. On Gonko's wave, Makail proceeded. Inside the twenty-foot square hut, it smelled like a dusty, abandoned warehouse built of cinder blocks. To the right, against the back wall was the kush, wide enough to take a quarter of the distance from wall to wall. In the left corner, a smaller bed awaited a child's night. Blankets piled high on the floor next to each bed. Along the back wall between the two beds, two layers of wooden racks held a variety of clothing. Coming closer to the entrance, a table with three wooden chairs rested in the center. Closest to the entrance, Makail noticed cabinets, wooden carvings of human faces and animals, as well as jewels and ancient gadgets that must have been passed down over generations. Nice home, Makail thought, as he grabbed one blanket from the heap, and curled himself into his most comfortable position on the larger kush, now feeling as hypnogogic as he'd acted.

Once Makail had settled in the hut, Gonko had walked to the opposite side of his village where his wife, Biantha watched their son, who tumbled around in the wet morning grass with only a couple other early-rising children. In height, Gonko didn't measure up to his wife; her more delicate and temperate flesh made her seem too fair for Gonko; her lighter, softer brown eyes had dazzled Gonko several years ago; and their kind hearts found great commonalities. Always a husband, father, and friend to all, Gonko stood beside his wife on this morning to tell her, "A young pale-fleshed man came upon our village this morning." She turned to him with not concern but attention. "He met me at the village limits, as I neared the end of my time on watch. He is a kind man, genuine. A lost man of Pithlyn, though. I directed him to our home, for he had meandered all night and now needs rest. We should not wake him. If we must enter our home today, we shall do so with calm eager."

"That's kind of you. Gontu and I will remain a distance from the home."

"Thank you. He also attained a horrendous wound on his side, so after dinner this evening, I will take him to heal." Gonko pecked his wife on her cheek and turned back toward the village, intending to prepare with his partners.

But Biantha halted him, "Before you go for your hunt today, you should speak with Ranwyn about this cheechako."

"You're right, my dearest. I will make him aware at once. Enjoy your day."

Ranwyn held the esteemed position of Endefder's authoritator. He oversaw everything in the village, ensuring each person fulfilled their role in society. Each person had a particular task to perform on a daily basis typically based on their families' reputation of a specific talent. A few men used a certain tool that had handles for each hand, a bar stretching from the handles to the bottom where a cylinder with welded blades and two wheels spun. The few men using this tool kept grass at a proper and acceptable level throughout the village and surrounding village limits. Each of these grass-cutting men had a helper who gathered the chopped grass blades to use for filling and refilling kush mattresses as a way of keeping them plump and comfortable. Others hunted, for food and clothing; some transformed the hunted into clothing; several built huts and made requested adjustments to standing huts; few served on guard; the responsibilities extend beyond the aforementioned. In brief, everybody worked for a common goal: continued progression of life.

Gonko, making his trek all the way back to the opposite side of town again, felt as though he may completely wear himself out before heading out for his day of hunting. Endefder expanded the equivalence of more than two miles from the first hut—the authoritators abode—to the last hut, where Gonko had spoken to his wife. Nevertheless, Gonko paused on the doorstep to Ranwyn's home. Quietly hesitating since nobody seemed to stir on the inside, Gonko knocked on the door.

After moments of nothing, footsteps crept slowly to the door, and Ranwyn creaked it open. "Gonko," he said with early-morning joy. "What brings you here so early? I thought you were heading out to hunt. Do you need more hunting supplies before you go?"

"Nothing like that, sir. I thought you should know of my recent encounter while finishing my watch duty."

"Were you harmed? Oh good Gracen, did anything happen to you? You look quite well."

"Nothing like that, sir. A man by the name of Makail

approached our village, so when he came near enough—"

Before he could finish, Ranwyn had directed his attention to the north in the same direction from where Makail had come. Gonko shifted his eyes for a moment to check if his authoritator gazed while listening or actually saw something. With his eye shift, he doubled, as a gate guard came hoofing, strangulating for air. More winded than Makail had appeared, this man arrived before Ranwyn and Gonko, imploring for the village authoritator.

"That's me, of course," Ranwyn insisted. "What is your trouble on this fine morning? Has there been an intruder? Has a guard turned on the rest of you? Oh, Gracen, is Pithlyn's wall falling down?"

"No—sir," drawing deep breaths between his words. "There has been a fire early this morning, just on the other side of Pithlyn's gates. We have tamed the flame, but there is great concern. Fires don't just begin out of nowhere, and we fear this is an act of Dymetrice, signaling a coming invasion. I've only come to warn you: be on the lookout for anything amiss."

"Thank you, kind guard," Ranwyn expressed. "We will watch over everything very tightly, especially my good man here, Gonko. He is set to hunt today with a few other men. They will watch for any unfamiliar faces."

With a farewell, the guard headed back to his position at a much slower pace than he'd employed on his trip down. Ranwyn turned attention back to Gonko, "When you hunt today, keep your eyes open for any other person who may have started the fire." He almost turned back to his home when remembering, "Oh, you had an encounter this morning?"

"Yes, I just wanted to inform you that a good soul from Fiwell stopped by, and I'm allowing him to sleep in my home for the day. He was up all night and must rest today. Biantha knows not to wake him."

"You have always been a kind man, Gonko. I will let any curious villager know."

"Thank you. I must ready myself for the day's hunt now." Gonko directed his body through the village. As he crossed his dwelling, he stared at the door for a few moments, wondering if the man on his bed had been completely honest, or was he of Dymetrice, starting a fire too close to the prominent land of the sphere? Gonko knew he must confront him with this before anybody else, before the healing. After all, Gonko would find truth in the healing methods.

Royal Duties

"My Queen, it is time to rouse," Fidelis requested from the doorway of her sprilen. Her oversized bed, centered in the room, towered over anybody who entered the room—more than seven feet high. Coming from the foot of the bed, a small staircase dropped to the ground. The ceiling rose twenty feet high, which held a smaller measurement than the length and width. Along the east wall opposite Fidelis, a window gave way for the sun's rays. She possessed no cabinets or drawers for clothing, as everything she wore hung in one of her three closets. A desk, however, rested underneath the window. At her desk, she studied potential guidelines for Pithlyn villages, notes from villages and other masses. She quietly retained order from this study, ensuring her people's happiness, allies remain friendly, and enemies never breach Pithlyn plains. On the west side of her bed closer to the doorway, a meeting table surrounded by chairs scuffed the floor. She'd utilize the table when meeting with Fidelis, Dux—leader of her committee—and others who may obtain valuable information. Fidelis stood motionless, grabbing his right wrist behind the small of his back, and he continued, "We have a long day today. We must grant royal order for village leaders of Pithly, Nearo, and Mofdar. They requested our attention many days ago, and we stated promptness."

She peeked her eyes toward the window, as the rising sun trickled through. She said aloud, "I've slept so well, but morning comes too soon."

"Let us not feel sorry for ourselves, my queen. We have high duties today. Our people depend on us," he replied with confidence and explicit order.

Bidellia stood atop her bed in a nightgown most in Pithlyn would wear for elegance. Stepping down from her bed she walked straight into her closet, changing into her queen's garb. When she set foot back into the room, Fidelis remained a stone figure, and Bidellia swiped her dazzling crown from a hidden slideout in the wall. Bidellia understood the importance of these village trips, for she knew her people counted on her and her closest advisors to present themselves appropriately upon request. She never took these lightly, and today would be no different; however, her mind traveled else place. She spoke, "But when the sun returns, we'll take our ride."

"Yes, my queen, tomorrow is empty, and we will take our ride to Favally, as you wish. Today, though, we must ride to the villages."

She beamed a shining smile, ignoring the last part of his comment, "Oh, what a truth! I ought to wake the moon, for sun's next rise shall set my soul aglide," and she lost herself in thought of finding her love.

Fidelis smirked toward his queen, "I'm glad you're confident in tomorrow's endeavor. Let us go on now—Pithly awaits."

She held a tender smile, sinking her forehead once before walking out her room into a large corridor, equivalent in height to her room. The sunlight gently painted the floors and walls with godly graces from the large ceiling windows. Continuing through her castle, she reached her throne room with Fidelis right behind her. She stared out the windows beyond her chair in the direction of Favally where the perfect man for her had to exist. As she came back to the present moment, she continued her thoughts aloud, "But first, today—the people need our view." Fidelis did not respond to her softly spoken words; rather, he followed her along the sapphire strip to the doors as high as Pithlyn's gates, where two lightly armored men held the handles ready to bring the day's air into the castle on Bidellia's nod. The doors slowly opened at her command and the golden rush of a morning sun illuminated the entire room.

Stepping outside, a set of rocky stairs declined four hundred feet to sea level where a slim stream ran south to north before bending through the mountains. To cross the stream, five from the queen's fleet of raxars waited next to the final step on a minute plain. Raxars were horse-like animals with longer more narrow snouts, resembling the shape of a crocodile. Where a horse's belly bulges, the raxar's body remained trim and muscular. Their legs ranged from three to four feet high with streaks of muscles ripping through hair. Unlike horses, the backs of a raxar's neck had no mane, but their tails draped thin long hairs, like a horse. The primary purpose of raxars was to endure long distances. They were bred to hold a gallop for an entire day, exceeding three hundred miles, with capabilities of repeating such a day indefinitely. Occasional water stops served as the only necessity for the raxars, and they'd graze the grasses by day's end.

Three raxars stood in a triangle; the two in front paralleled each other six feet apart with a large carriage between them strapped to their backs and around their bellies. The third raxar supported the rear of this carriage, as padded girders stemmed back to him, hooking around his body. Fidelis, as always, grabbed

Chapter 6

the movable wooden staircase, which buckled under the base of the carriage. He swung it to the ground for Bidellia to enter her royal coach, and she nodded her head towards him as a show of appreciation. The front side of the coach arched to a point, peaking taller than Bidellia. This opening allowed Bidellia to keep an eye on the forthcoming. From the top of the opening, it bubbled to the back, enclosing along the base, and the chair inside replicated her throne.

Fidelis took his place on the raxar to the right of Bidellia's configuration. To her left, another lightly armored guard rode along with an attachment to his raxar, straggling several feet behind on small wheels was a cubed cage fit for at least half a dozen men. Fidelis and the guard's raxars moved first to lead the way. As the raxars spattered across the stream, water hardly rose to dampen their undersides. Beyond the stream, a field of flowers covered the terrain except for a wide alleyway for royal journeys. The flowery meadow extended a couple miles from the mountain range, and ended with an infrequent arrangement of trees. Clearing past the trees, however, they arrived to the large village of Pithly, the mass's leading, most heavily populated village, separated by less than four miles from the castle.

When they entered the boundary of Pithly, three men waited. These three men led the village, making them next in line for the royal committee in the event of a death or other mishap within the current committee. One of the men stood in front of the other two, presenting himself as the authoritator. As the five raxars stopped immediately to the fore of this man, he called out, "Greetings Your Royalness, from Pithly. My name is Soren, I am the High Authoritator within these boundaries, and we have anxiously anticipated your arrival. There is a thief among us in Pithly, and we have thinned it to three suspects. A closer review of our suspects by the highest confidence in all the land will bring forth the absolute perpetrator. Thank you for allowing us your time."

Fidelis responded on behalf of the royal party. "It is with great dignity that we come to you. Thieving is not accepted in our land, and we will take great measures to assure the many honest people here will see justice prevail and security restored."

"It is appreciated fine sir. Follow us to where we have our prospective illmates shackled and prepared for scrutiny." They traveled around the town's huts, as residents watched, catching a glimpse of the highest queen in the sphere. On the opposite outskirt of the village, the three suspects waited for the deliberations to begin. The suspects stood on a platform, which had a railing between them and the chain-link constraints dangling from their wrist to their ankles. Vertical wooden pillars from rail to base prevented the suspects from overlapping.

Soren began describing the situation on each, referring to them respectively as Suspect One, Suspect Two, and Suspect Three. Each of them live alone, without a companion or child. They each perform good deeds within the town. Suspect One weaves containers from shaven strips of wood so his fellow Pithly neighbors can organize belongings; Suspect Two meanders through town ascertaining happiness for all in the community; and Suspect Three sharpens blades, whether necessary for a sword, tool for a craft, or blade to shave hairs from the skin. But they are suspected of the crime for recent reactions toward those who have carped of something stolen. Seven people had met with Soren, explaining of missing possessions. The list contained the likes of men's attire, golden necklaces, knives, and food supplies. Each of these men advised the word not to get out because it could harm the good name of Pithly. And, each of these suspects have chattered of moving to another village to begin anew. Lastly, Soren stated that he believes a search is in order, but such an act is prohibited without the queen's order.

After hearing the stories, Fidelis questioned the men individually because if any of them lied to his high position, they would face a greater offense than petty theft. He reported his results to Bidellia, declaring that none of them claim themselves a thief, and the only way to find the man who had lied and stolen would require further investigate. Bidellia agreed, and she looked toward Soren, commanding, "We'll search their huts."

They rode through the paths of Pithly with Soren leading the way, as he knew the dwellings of each man. The first suspect's hut stored few possessions, as Fidelis browsed through everything. He came back to the Bidellia, announcing Suspect One holds nothing matching the description of the stolen. Suspect Two lived in a larger residence, and again, Fidelis entered first. When he came back to the queen, he dropped the staircase before saying, "You must see this, my queen." She nodded her head, and stepped from her chair to enter the home in question. The two scanned the room, disbelieving any thief would appear so open within the confines of his own dwelling. Four golden necklaces, piles of men's clothing, a collection of knives, and they could safely assume he'd already tucked the food into his belly. Queen Bidellia looked to Fidelis and affirmed, "We've found the man of fault."

The royal party returned to the zone of inquiry. Soren released Suspect One from his shackles and stated quietly, "I am sorry for the misunderstanding dear friend.

We had to snare the man causing damage to our village. We have held you captive for an offense done by another man. You are free, and I thank you for your honesty. Please do not hold these acts against the village, for we will compensate for our error." He released Suspect Three, declaring the same. Soren fronted Suspect Two, and said, "You have committed a horrible misdeed, and you will now reside in our detaining cell for a long time."

Overhearing this, Fidelis interrupted: "No, he will not remain in Pithly. He lied to the face of the Royal Committee. He will dwell in our dungeon."

"Very well," Soren responded.

The royal guard, Fidelis, and Soren, unlocked the iniquitous man's feet and escorted him to the cage connected to the guard's raxar. The guard took him alone at the cage, shoving him into his temporary home. The guard ensued to grab the prisoner by the hands so that he could be latched from ankle to hands again, much as he'd been when the two first met earlier in the morning.

On the ride to Nearo, not a lengthy distance northeast of Pithly, Fidelis led the way, centering himself between the two front raxars hoisting the queen while the guard hung back to the left of Bidellia's carriage; this way Bidellia would not have to see the illmate every moment for the remainder of their expedition. However, she could hear the prisoner, speaking to the guard, as the guard continued to silence him. From portions of the bantering, she found the man had called himself Cil, as opposed to Suspect Two or illmate. Before arriving to Nearo, they stopped at Vafarm, an agricultural village, with plains of crops stretching for miles. Vafarm supplied the castle with all of its produce and commonly provided dairy and meats to supplement what the illmates hunted. Vafarm's authoritator, or supervisor of crops and animals, wanted to harvest the royal group with only the best meal he could offer through trembling hands.

In Nearo, the village's authoritator iterated the scarcity of food source in a nearby wilderness. He expressed his concern that loyal inhabitants of Pithlyn's more distant villages have swept through depleting a once rampant wilderness, which had long been the sole source of meat for their entire community. Fidelis questioned the man on his solution, as no village is to bring a concern to royal awareness without a proposed resolution. The authoritator exclaimed his case of prohibiting any man to enter, faulting the beautiful residents of Nearo the vigor to survive. By the end of his statement, Bidellia rose from her chair, "Verboten Faults," deeming a new title for the wilderness, "no guest is welcomed through."

The sun began its descent to the western horizon, as the royal unit moved at an angle to the north and west from Nearo to Mofdar, which claimed the longest travel of the day. Queen Bidellia spent most of the journey in thought with hopes of sighting the perfect man for her during the expedition commencing tomorrow. She anticipated him as bold, unwavering, with the courage to stand up and speak to her as if she hadn't the highest throne in the entire sphere while also demonstrating the respect and courtesy such a queen deserves. Oh, her feelings beat from her soul as her smile couldn't fade. She would find her soul's sole missing glory when morning comes.

The raxars stopped, cracking Bidellia's mindset. The authoritator of Mofdar greeted Fidelis, glanced nervously to the queen who sat within her shell, "Greetings Your Royalness," he called, receiving a closed smile and a head nod. The problem in Mofdar revolved around a man who would not let the children engage in recreation among children. He constantly interfered with their games, even going so far as to knocking them down or ridiculing their inferiority. The flawed man positioned himself as the village's builder, and always helped with projects around the town. He came off as a good man, but has taken matters too far with the children. Children play with children, and adults either spectate, or remain occupied with tasks. His proposed resolution involved overthrowing the man from the village, but the queen had a better idea, "Eschew the man!" she ordered. No person of Mofdar would ever again acknowledge his existence, and when children play, they shall move their games continuously to counter his interference.

With duties concluded for the queen's long day, they enjoyed a serene ride back. Cil had stopped barking at the guard, and the guard no longer antagonized Cil. The Queen stepped back into the thoughts from earlier, feeling she'd been alone for far too many revolutions. But just the notion of having that perfect match kept her thriving. As the raxars spattered through the shallow stream, she stared upward toward her castle. The front wall stretched from one mountain face to the next; the doors looked like giants dwelled; and the staggered elevation of the roof's depth resembled a staircase to Gracen, as it vanished to a separation in the mountains, revealing a bright hue from the stunning sunset, as a pink blaze blasted low, clouding upward to the darkness of night. And all she could think was beyond her royal committee, she had nobody with whom she could share this.

As the raxars stopped, she looked to Fidelis and said, "Before the dusk we halt," approving the efficiency of their duties today.

"Yes, justice reigned supreme on this day. The good fortunes of Pithlyn rest within their timeless queen," he complimented.

She smiled in acceptance, as the two walked up the mountainous steps toward the doors. The guard guided the shackled offender up the stairs more than ten steps behind them. When the doors opened on the queen's command, the guard turned the man to the right. Cil stumbled, unable to grip proper footing on the inclined terrain, all the way to a door in the ground. The guard opened this door and followed Cil down the stairway. He disengaged the chain restraints on Cil, before thrusting him into a barred cell.

In the main entryway to the castle, Fidelis started hassling the queen of the men with whom they'd come in contact throughout the day. "Surely there must have been one kind man today who met your fancy, like Soren of Pithly?"

The queen simply shook her head with a look that called Fidelis ridiculous, so he pressed, "You have no mind to consider a man of Pithlyn as an appropriate counterpart for you. What might be so wrong with the men of our righteous land? Do you not love the men here?" Though he'd said the questions aloud, they were more of a thought for him to ponder in privacy, but the queen heard his questioning quite clearly.

She responded, as if Fidelis's remark had been absurd, "My, yes, I love the ones who walk my grass," hesitating before continuing disheartedly, "And all these men have quivered at my thumb."

Healing

Makail awoke before sundown. Startled upon the first flicker of his eyes, he quickly realized where he'd slept. He sat on the kush, swinging his feet to the floor. He stood and stretched his arms over his head, before walking outside where Gonko and his family spoke with another family nearby. Makail stared in their direction until Gonko noticed him. Acknowledging his presence, Gonko lifted an open palm above his wife's head then used it to motion Makail his way. Makail complied with the request and began an even walk to the gathering.

"This is my old friend, Makail," Gonko told the circle. "He has made many travels in his life, but this land, Pithlyn, is his home. We welcome him and invite him to remain in our village as long as he desires." Turning his attention to Makail, he introduced, "This is my wife, Biantha and our child, Gontu." Biantha ensued to lightly shake Makail's hand as a welcoming gesture. A friend of her husband's was always a friend of hers and their son.

"It's nice to meet you, and I thank you for allowing me to find rest within your home. I appreciate it very much," Makail said.

Biantha replied to him in a dulcet voice, "It is our duty to ensure the health and strength of Pithlyn men are preserved."

"And to further show assurance of your health and strength," Gonko interupted, "we invite you to our nightly spread."

Makail nodded his head, knowing he could not turn down such an offer since his last meal came in the form of fish from the previous night. The two families before him headed to the spread, and Makail followed. They made a right at the first intersection, not shifting left until the path ended with the last line of huts. While on the southbound path, Gonko drifted back to meet with Makail, asking if Makail had slept well.

"Yes, thank you for not waking me earlier," Makail replied.

"That was not a problem, compé." Gonko paused before continuing, "I was thinking while you rested, and I have a question for you." Makail looked to him with curious eyes, and Gonko asked, "What brings you to the vicinity of our village?"

"My travels had taken me to Dymetrice, Quintix Valley specifically," Makail began his fabrication. "Several days ago, as I walked near the coast hunting a grilk, this unthinkable wave hovered toward me. I couldn't see it until there was no time for me to move far enough away from the coast, so I dove toward the wave, hoping it could ride atop until the fierce undertow whipped me through the deep and brought me to the surface again." Gonko stared at him in amazed disbelief. "The wave suctioned me to the top and washed me toward the valley before sucking me back under and spitting me out in the Gelid Deep. I was under water for quite some time, but I have trained my chest to endure lengths without breathing. Then I just started to swim. The sun rose four times during my swim, but I knew I couldn't stop. That would mean the end of my life. The first land my eyes could see was the east side of the northern coast here, and then I just started walking south after reaching the land. So the bruise on my side is actually from the wave thrusting me into a very stiff, heavy object before taking me further. I'm sorry for the previous fib, I just didn't think you would believe the truth."

"I don't know what to believe," Gonko said, "That's an extraordinary story."

Healing

"I know. My grand fortunes have kept me alive. Does your village have a name?" Makail quickly changed the subject.

"Yes, this is Endefder. We are the easternmost village in Pithlyn, making us defenders of this land against the nemesis beyond Threatle Gap. And you are welcome to train with us, a daily routine here. We must always be prepared for an enemy's storm."

"I will consider your offer," Makail said. "Before you allowed me to sleep here today, you said you would show me great healing. Is the food we are soon to eat what you meant by the healing?"

"No compé. When we finish nourishing, I will take you to the place." "There was a fire this morning."

"In the village?" Makail played the tune of innocence and unknowing.

"No—outside the gates. You are unaware of this blaze?" he speculated.

Promptly, "Yes. How did it come about?"

"The gate's guards are unsure, and they worry it may be a prelude to worse."

"We should rest to hope it stirred erroneously. I'm sure it's nothing."

The families in front of Makail and Gonko had chatted with steps until the dwellings discontinued where rows of wooden tables covered the grass. Beyond the tables, flames brushed through the breeze with a variety of meats above them, which filled the air with a Memorial Day barbeque smell. Many families formed lines as children ran around, chasing each other with smiles on their faces. But the most spectacular view in all of this was the mountainous horizon. Since Makail had lived within a mountain range so much of his life, he never had the opportunity to step back and view mountains' beauty from afar. Although these mountains didn't escalate as high as those of Quintix Valley, the way they hugged closely made it appear like a stronger cluster. At such a distance, 150 miles, the mountains steamed a hazy sun-splashed orange tint, adding to their wonder.

Food filled the length of three long tables. Preparers had cut meat slight enough to form sampler platters and berries and vegetables looked too fresh and clean to eat. Makail loaded his dish with grilk, turnobings, fish, berries, and two different vegetables. He sat with Gonko and his family who interacted with the surrounding families during dinner. Makail silently observed them, obtaining a feel for the way of life in this village, as he felt it would be similar in many ways to other villages in Pithlyn. Gonko controlled most of the talking while Biantha smiled and nodded with few words. The children ate quietly with exquisite manners, dabbing their mouths with cloth after every bite, keeping elbows off the table, responding kindly when asked questions, and using appropriate utensils, which included a dully edged knife and an isosceles triangle—like a miniature pie cutter—used to stab meat or scoop vegetable. Makail thought the children were most remarkable. They ran and played as children often do, but once they sat at the table it was like they were eating before royalty.

"Did you have enough to eat?" Gonko asked after Makail had cleared his dish.

"I did. It was an excellent meal, and I thank you for allowing me to eat with you, your family, and your village."

"Then we will go," Gonko said abruptly as he stood from the bench, leaving his half-eaten dish on the table. "Biantha, I will take him to heal that wound he's endured. I will be back, but there is no need to wait up for me; we may be late."

Biantha nodded to her husband while Makail rose to his feet. Makail looked down to his empty plate and Gonko's mess. "How do we go about discarding the remains of our meals?" he asked.

"That will be taken care of, compé. You need not worry of that," Gonko replied.

At Gonko's words, the two walked away silently with Makail trailing left by half a step. Gonko did not lead him back through the village; instead, they headed northwest toward the front of the village, only wide to the west of any dwellings. By the time they came in line with the north entrance of Endefder, Gonko turned directly west. The sporadic trees through which Makail had walked in the early morning persisted, clumping together more and more as they continued. In the thickening woods, Makail shifted toward Gonko, asking "Where exactly do you take me, compé?" Gonko's response begged of patience, for he knew the destination, and he wanted Makail to blindly trust him. "We will be there once the wood breaks."

"How far is that?" Makail wondered.

"No farther than we have already come."

They continued through the forest, and the day began to darken. The forest's quaggy terrain became stickier than the ground closer to Endefder. In a few areas, thin water caught their feet and mud fumed through a feeble wind, but the two continued on their way. Makail, in the muck, thought about the intentions of his voyage to Pithlyn. Being alone with Gonko presented the perfect time to ask Gonko a few questions. Dodging low-drooping branches and tree stumps, Makail asked, "Could you tell me something about the lady, Bidellia?"

Gonko stopped, turning to face Makail with inquisitive eyes. "You mean our queen?" Gonko retorted, feeling the Highest had just been disrespected, belittled to the level of a common madam.

Makail stood with a blank expression, thinking, *the queen? My mother and father sent me here expecting the queen to keep me safe?* His voice, however, remained calm and confident. "Yes, our queen. Queen Bidellia."

Gonko turned to continue guiding Makail through the trees toward their target. Keeping his eyes forward, Gonko spoke, "What is it you don't already know about our queen?"

"Well," Makail began carefully, "I've never met her, but I know she's been the Queen of Pithlyn for a length. Truthfully, I hardly know much of our queen. Anything you could share with me would be helpful."

Gonko started with the basics, sustaining their traveling pace. "She has been our queen for more than five hundred years. She is the only immortal this sphere has ever known. By immortal, I do mean nothing can end her. If she were struck by sword, the sword would shatter on her skin. If a mountain crumbled, engulfing her, she would slither from under unscathed. Of course, a mountain could not actually crumble, but you understand my thoughts." Gonko peered back to see Makail staring at him and nodding his head. "She has led men to battle hundreds of times and has never come out in defeat. She has a keen sense of compromise, and settles issues with spoken words rather than excessive bloodshed. She understands battle comes from disagreements. To her, the point of a battle is to resolve disputes, not to kill man. Deaths will never bring one side closer to an agreement…unless the death is royal, I suppose.

"She is a kind queen. She loves her people, and when a commune has a problem, she visits them with the noble party to reach a solution. She has even come to Endefder, granting us an arsenal of weaponry to protect the land from enemy swarms, even though our village is a twenty-day journey from her mountain castle." Gonko simply resumed describing everything he knew of his queen, and Makail listened intently, flabbergasted by the notions of such a being. "She will stretch her love to great lengths to assure camaraderie throughout the entire mass of Pithlyn. She wants no village to feel royal neglect, and her ultimate triumph will be for all the lands to spend their loyalties with her. Not because she wants control, but she knows there is no person fairer than she." Gonko pressed his lips together and cut his stride slowly in half. "And this," spreading his arms, palms up, at waist level, "is how she preserves the strength of all her beloved people in Pithlyn."

Makail drew even with Gonko, scanning from the north to the south. He saw nothing of great importance until he saw Gonko's eyes looking toward the ground.

Makail saw the flowers. Directly in front of them were deep blue flowers, the darkest in the range. As Makail budged his view to the right, the colors faded, spreading to royal blue, baby blue, and the palest of blues before the white flowers of the core, ensuing to reflect the pattern of colors pale to deep. "You brought me to a prairie of flowers?"

Sensing doubt, Gonko asked, "How deep is your pain?"

"It feels worse than this morning. There's a swollen tightness surrounding my ribs, like the strike ruptured my structure."

"Come," Gonko stepped past Makail, motioning him to follow, trotting along a strip of grass between trees and flowers. When Gonko stopped, he reached down and delicately plucked a baby blue flower while Makail watched with his mouth ajar. As the flower's roots ripped from the ground another stem broke through, growing as quickly as the other flower ascended, and blooming into a baby blue flower of the same height as the rest. Makail had never seen anything happen like that.

Makail remained unsure of what Gonko was doing? "I know we're newfound friends, but you really didn't need to go picking flowers for me, and I don't see how this will help my sore side."

Chapter 7

"Ah, have your doubts, compé, but this method has never failed. Raise your shirt." Makail fulfilled the request, and Gonko individually peeled the pedals from the flower. With each pedal, he gently pressed them over Makail's wound. To Makail's surprise, the flower piece stuck to his side like dampened paper. Gonko kept his focus on the wound, despite Makail's consistent head shaking. He covered the bruise entirely with the single flower's pedals. Holding the empty stem, Gonko placed it back on the soil beneath the other flowers before pressing both palms to Makail's tender, flower-covered area. In one swoop, he swiped each pedal off Makail's side, revealing a skin tone matching the rest of his body without a sign of any harm.

Makail widened his eyes, "There's no swelling, no pain."

"There's no mark."

"How?" Makail invited, bewildered by the fact a flower just suctioned to his skin and healed his wound within seconds. He couldn't find more words in his amazement.

"There are three regions of the flowers in Pithlyn. Queen Bidellia called on the Goddess of Healing, Medeal a few hundred years ago after Dymetrice brutalized many of her men, including a man she thought she'd loved. The Dymetrice army retreated shortly after, and Bidellia asked in kindness for Medeal to bring great healing to her land for, hoping this would help revitalize her men, even keep her love alive. Medeal allowed for these flowers to spring, and many men were healed and ready to defend Pithlyn once more. Some suffered great harm and could not be brought back, not because the flowers didn't work, but because the flowers came after the blood had stopped flowing. Most importantly, the pedals only cling to Pithlyn flesh. On a man of any other land, the pedal would slide off and float to the ground. I can never be too sure of one's origin since the Goddess of Tounge has given Prodigion a common language, but these flowers assure a man is of Pithlyn blood."

Impressed by the story, Makail said, "You sure know the history of our land. A lot better than me. Maybe I should stop all my travels and discover more on the remarkable history of Pithlyn."

"There is much to discover, compé. But you are healed now, so we must go back," Gonko insisted.

"Wait," Makail stopped him. "You said for the noble party to reach Endefder, it is a twenty-day journey. Where exactly does that journey begin?"

"Another history lesson?"

"If you wish it to be, then share your depths," Makail pleaded.

"In the year of zero, 538 years ago, Bidellia verged on

becoming the queen of Pithlyn. She was the swiftest in the land with a sword but swifter with words. She led many legions of men into battle. Her abilities with sword and word allowed her to speak with the Highest from other masses. In the last battle between Pithlyn and Favally, Bidellia scurried to the King of Favally and sought allegiance, pressing that as allies, the two masses could do more and be greater. The king countered with one request for an alliance to be reached. Pithlyn had to make her the Queen. Because Favally was the reason she took the throne, she had her castle erected between the twin mountains, which pose identical gantor peaks. These twin mountains rest in the southernmost part of our western mountains, right next to Pithlyn Pass, which leads to Favally. We've now built a golden wall before Pithlyn Pass, and her words to the king are carved into it."

"I will never doubt your wealth of knowledge," Makail said while the two remained next to the flowers. "Is there a way I could travel there from here without being seen?"

"Do you not plan to continue in Endefder?"

"You have been very kind to me, as has your entire village. I am grateful for everything you have shared with me and everything you have done for me. But I must continue on my way. I'm sorry."

"My best wishes will walk beside you. Now, why would it matter if you're seen?"

Makail had an untruth ready for that question, "In my travels to view the castle, I would like to arrive most quickly. Therefore, I would rather not be stopped by any of the kind people of our land, as that would distract me from my journey."

"I see. It is a long journey anyway," Gonko began. Roughly 3500 miles separated Pithlyn's east and west coasts. "It may help you to visit with the villages for rest along the way. But there is no safe route, as you describe. Our people may meander wherever they please. And I must warn you there is a wide river running north and south, our Pithlyn River, and it is very difficult to navigate. If you choose to swim, it will take you half the day, and the current will drift you south, but there are three bridges across this bridge. One is just north of a straight line from here, another is very much more north, but the one to the south lines up perfectly with the Pithlyn Palace."

"Thank you for that advice and all you've done."

"You are welcome. Please, visit Endefder in your later journeys. I will be pleased to see you again."

The two maintained eye contact before bidding a final farewell. Makail watched Gonko fade back into the woods, and he began walking north along the path by the flowers. Making his way around the flowers, he saw a vast open field sloping upward from his position. As he wlaked west, the open field of beautifully maintained grass gradually increased its rise. Reaching the plateau, he looked back at the splendid scene, as a long expanse slowly sunk to a forest with Medeal's flowers corning the expanse. He felt like a king overseeing his glorious region.

Turning to continue his trail to the queen's castle, he grappled through a thickening wood. As the trees cleared, he saw another village in his short distance. He thought briefly of what to do then bolted south, hooking his direction westerly to aim a straight path for Pithlyn River.

Meet Bidellia

As the woods cleared, Makail searched the night for any wanderers. With nothing coming into his view, he blistered through the open fields, the farms, the timberlands, over the rolling hills, past the villages, eclipsing the pace he regularly ran in Quintix Valley. While zooming past everything in his bare feet, he could feel a softness in the terrain, and he could see a calmness in his phantasmagoric surroundings. The calmness swathed the blurring land not because of the serenity that overcomes a village as the people rest, but because Queen Bidellia's reign obliged an air of tranquility. She ruled with such dignity and pride, love and care, honor and admirableness that her protection resonated into peace through her land. Makail, though he'd only footed Pithlyn soil for a slumbered day, could feel the effects of a righteous ruler, and he couldn't wait to take his first

Chapter 9

glance of her. The thought consumed him as he ran; mainly, what will she look like?

Through the darkness, he could see ahead of him enough to give himself time to react. At his speed, his eyesight remained of utter importance. Though his speed marked blinding measures, he kept aware of his next move. And he could see the broad waterway ahead of him with enough time to think, I could head south and find that bridge since that would direct me on a straight path to Queen Bidellia's castle. Queen, I still can't believe my parents sent me here to meet the queen. Oh me. I could just jump! Without breaking stride, he dashed through the air over the four miles of unsteady midnight blue. Continuing the running motion during a leap allowed him to land and seamlessly hold his roaring pace. He never slowed a beat, maintaining focus on his destination. By the time mountains amused his horizon, the moon lingered closely above, and Makail knew light would soon shed the land. He also knew the mountains ahead would guide him to the Highest.

As the ground began to rise and dip, Makail, for the first time since he'd started running on the other side of the mass, slowed his speed, coming to a coasting halt at the base of a mountain. He inhaled deeply followed by a sharp exhale. He'd made it before morning. To find the castle, Gonko mentioned she built it in the mountains.

Thus, Makail ran between the mountains' bases, making an effort to turn himself south as much as the mountain would allow. As he'd set himself appropriately due south, he charged upward, running as if he were back in Quintix Valley, except he would not let himself waste the time of reaching the summit. Instead, once he ran high enough, he'd bound toward the next mountain, landing on each with the pliability of a cat. This made his journey trickier, and his focus revolved around the precision of each jump—when to leap, how far, where to land. He didn't even notice the castle to his left when he completely passed it. Eventually, the mountains became shorter until he ran over them like hills. In his distance, he saw a golden gate, like the one through which he'd snuck yesterday morning. He continued running toward it, hoping it might give him a sense of where he needs to go. To his left, he noticed a long light-colored, like sand, wood fence, which had posts every six feet with three beams connecting each post. He couldn't see where the fence ended, but where it began stood a massive dark brown ranch. Several creamy brown raxars bowed their heads, sniffing the ground, just outside of the ranch. Makail considered the size of the structure; there must have been a hundred or so raxars inside.

Redirecting his attention, he arrived at the gate, recognizing it as a Pithlyn gate but without guards. No door existed on this wall, only a tall, wide opening, encouraging people to come and go. Confused by the contrast, Makail aimlessly scanned the wall, while feeling its texture. To the right of the doorway, on the gold of the wall, set a flat stone no larger than Makail's torso. On this stone, a lapidary expression read:

At battle, only greatest men are slain.
Together, we could have the best of all
With land and water heaping for our reign,
And legions, oh so mighty, others fall.
And more! Let fighting cease for both to win,
As we can reap, as one, a sovereign kin.
-Queen Bidellia

Makail realized this had to be the wall to Pithlyn Pass, leading to Favally. Gonko had mentioned this. He'd also said the queen had to build her castle close. Makail twisted his head over his right shoulder, slightly swiveling his body, examining the first tall mountain of the range just beyond the grassy hills. That one ought to be close enough, he thought.

He searched his surroundings as the sun began to fracture the eastern horizon. Not a person wandered near him, so he carried a tremendous, yet slower speed back over the hills. When he set foot on the mountain, he hushed his pace even more and stayed on the east side of the mountain this time. And there it was, nestled on a crevice caused by the divergence of one double-peaking mountain. His aerial view revealed a giant square with stems at the front streaming south a short distance, north for a greater distance, and equivalent to the width of the square, the castle gorged deepest to the west. A narrow stub also poked toward the east, which spilled into rocky steps. At the bottom of the steps, he saw a grassy aisle, then a slim stream, followed by the same flowers to which Gonko had taken him, except these had a wide strip of grass down the middle with the whitest flowers on either side.

Inside the castle, Queen Bidellia woke up excited, reminiscent of how one wakes on the first morning of vacation. Unlike yesterday, nobody had come to her door, but she knew what this sunrise would bring, and she had never been so giddy over something so ridiculous. In a frenzy, she readied herself for the day then stormed out her door. Fidelis heard her knock at his door, so he quickly flung the door open. Seeing his appealing queen, he said he will only be a moment. Bidellia nodded with an enthusiastic smile then stepped quickly to the main entry room and paced in front of her throne. When Fidelis joined her in the room, he said, "Your carriage awaits." Unable to restrain her anticipation, she ran after his words, leaving Fidelis to slowly follow. The two guards opening the doors to the castle whisked them open quicker than ever because of her scurry. She burst into the sunlight, charging down the steps, and Makail had positioned himself perfectly on that narrow eastern stub of the castle behind one of the pillars where he could view her for the first time.

He stared and noticed her from foot to face. She held the stature of a goddess' grace with slender features arms and legs and waist. The splendor of her eyes could ease a gaze—blue eyes to light a flameless room ablaze, and blondest hair, which kept her neck encased then floating to the mid of back in waves. Her smile, her shining smile with lips he craves to frame the whitest teeth the sun's embraced, which cause the smile to melt the soul of all. Her softest, fairest skin could never pall. Poetic beauty of the finest taste. She holds the beauty one could not digest, as she's perfection at perfection's best.

Fidelis caught up to her next to the raxars, which had aligned similarly to the day before, only facing the opposite direction. He pulled the steps down for Bidellia to step into her carriage. She beamed from dimple to dimple, and Fidelis hopped on his raxar to guide the way, centering himself in front of Bidellia's two lead raxars. Fidelis began the trip directly south, not crossing the stream. Makail noted the direction of the two, and zoomed toward the gates where he stopped about a mile from the gold. Fidelis and Bidellia would pass the mountain then stroll through the hills for a clear view of the exquisite Pithlyn Wall. From there, it would be a half day's journey across Pithlyn Pass to reach the Fence of Favally. While bumping through the hills, Fidelis explained to Bidellia that he had the head guard assign one of the guards to ride into Trilox, the third village in Favally, to request a quarters for the night. The authoritator had agreed, so the two of them would rest in the primary hut for that evening.

Still in the dawn of this excursion, the two declined the final slope of the hills when Fidelis noticed a man standing in their path. Squinting, he perceived the man's apparel and turned back toward Bidellia. "My queen," he shouted, "there is a man obstructing our course, and he wears the green of a former Dymetrice faction." Lips tight, she nodded, indicating her desire to continue past the man. As their approach grew closest, the man raised his right hand, wishing for the tandem to stop. "Do not halt us. We have royal obligations to fulfill, and you will not stand in our way," Fidelis announced.

"My name is Makail," he said boldly, "and I have traveled from Dymetrice to live safely under Queen Bidellia." Makail knew he could not start with lies if Bidellia were to keep him safe; therefore, he did not hide his mass of birth.

"There is no time for nonsense!" Fidelis exclaimed.

"No Dymetrice man seeks comfort in Pithlyn. Your idiocy is unwelcomed here."

The raxars stopped so Fidelis could ridicule Makail without intentions of delaying much further, but Makail had more to say. "This is far from nonsense, kind sir. I've come seeking the protection of Queen Bidellia, and I've come from far, far away. I cannot let myself be stopped by you when I'm so close to my inherited directive."

Fidelis felt his face quiver and teeth clinch. He turned back to his queen, "Is your wish to have this man killed?"

Bidellia stood in her sphere and looked to Makail, ruggedly handsome, a strong young man, then she looked to Fidelis, "Kill?" she questioned in a softly stunned voice. "Purge this man!" Directing her attention to Makail, she declared, "I'm queen of Pithlyn Mass." Makail shortly nodded his head, giving half a bow while Queen Bidellia continued to speak to Fidelis, "and he's no more than some Dymetrice scum."

"My queen," Fidelis injected while Makail stared with a hanging mouth, "with all my respect, that will set our journey back."

Interrupting, Makail cried, "You mustn't purge me! I have come too far."

"Quiet you insignificant dupe!" Fidelis retorted. He

turned again to Bidellia, "Are you sure you want wasted time on this," jousting an open palm toward Makail.

Bidellia nodded, "I'll have Makail escorted to the bleak."

"Then I shall take him," Fidelis agreed, revealing disgust in his tone, "but you continue on, and I will catch up briefly." Drawing his raxar close enough to Makail, he dismounted to land next to him. Fidelis took a long rope that tucked around the raxar's harness, keeping it secure. After confiscating Makail's sword, he used the rope to tie Makail's hands together while he begged for a reason why they're taking him away. To every bellow, Fidelis responded with a sharp "close it." Beyond words, Makail showed little resistance for two reasons: this may allow Fidelis to think he is weak and incapable of protecting himself, which meant Fidelis would underestimate him; and Queen Bidellia, the person he'd come so far to meet, ordered it. Finally, Fidelis had Makail firmly knotted and fastened to the saddle, dangling behind the raxar. As Fidelis, rode past Bidellia, he said, "This man's name does not deserve your breath, my queen."

Thudding over the hills again as Makail dragged behind, thumping the ground continuously. Fidelis gave Makail the most painful of rides he'd ever experienced. After the first hill, Fidelis pierced the air with a shrilling whistle, calling on any guard within earshot. Out of recognition, two guards watching over the castle from the outside hopped on raxars to check on the happenings. As they reached Fidelis, cutting his retreat nearly in half, Fidelis said, "This scum is of Dymetrice and impeded our progress. The queen's order is that he suffers in the dungeon."

"Then we will take him from here," the first guard said while the other untied Makail from Fidelis's raxar and secured him to their own. The remaining tumble to the castle slewed along more easily than the racing of Fidelis, who'd rushed back to reach the queen. The guards pulled him slowly without haste, as they spoke back and forth about where to put this new illmate. Already, twelve of the fifteen chambers held a scandalous soul, but one of the three open, unoccupied chambers, farthest to the north in the row of fifteen, lay directly beneath the bed of Queen Bidellia. With a sense of humor, the guards felt it appropriate to place Makail there since he'd probably impeded the queen's progress in an attempt to meet her. Resting under her with an impenetrable layer between them ought to drive a man insane.

Makail did not take kindly to this punishment of incarceration, keeping his feelings inside, except for his boiling skin. He turned red with anger. He sought the queen for protection, for her to keep him safe—not to send him to a dungeon. Is this what his parents had meant? He'll remain safe in the dungeon of the Pithlyn Palace? Makail knew he could escape easily from the two guards, but he knew, after all, they led him to the queen's castle, where he might have a chance to prove his worth, even if he's restrained to an isolated cube. Surely he'd think of something.

The two guards came to a stop at the bottom of the rocky steps. They jumped to the ground in unison, each grabbing one of Makail's arms to lead him up the stairs with hands still knotted together. As the three approached the castle, Makail inhaled the view. A marvelously constructed castle. The white wall seemed to crash into the mountain to the left. Right of the door extended all the way to the next of nature's incline. Near the end of that wall to the north, Makail could see a large overhang with more surface space than he'd had in his Quintix Valley dwelling. Atop the castle wide cylinders held up gold cones, pointing to the ski. On the tip of each cone waved the Pithlyn Pennant—a long, narrowing, deep blue isosceles triangle with a wide baby blue stripe from top to bottom near the flagpole.

Just before reaching the giant doors to the castle, the guards whipped Makail off the steps to walk through the harsh terrain toward the cellar door. Makail's bare feet scratched the ramshackle path as he appeared feeble and exhausted. His only true feeling, however, simmered as frustration. He played the tune of weakness, of course, so the guards would not feel he warrants special attention beneath the cellar doors which lay directly in front of them now. One guard pushed the shrubbery away from the doors, swinging them outward, opening a stretched staircase, while the other held both of Makail's arms. The guard who had opened the doors led the way, while the other cleaved behind Makail, assuring no escape.

At the stairs' base, the first aspect to catch Makail's attention was the horrid smell, like sweaty men and bodily waste. A short narrow floor jutted to a wide open room with torches lit, two on the side walls and four on the back wall. Two tables set symmetrically with two guards at each table. On each side of the narrow entry, black bars lined the walls, seven on each side of the entry, separated by a single layer of cinder block-like bricks, and each with the same-sized cell behind them. These holding rooms stretched deeper than wide, and Makail realized his rest would come in such quarters. As he looked in disgust at the men behind bars, the guard shouted to the men at the tables, "This imbecile tried stopping the queen! Last one," referring to which cell he'd occupy. Receiving head nods from the guards watching the other scoundrels, he forced Makail to the right from their entry all the way to the very end. After passing the seventh cell from their entry, the guard continued to shove Makail along until they reached the end of the hall where the wall was the mountain's side. The guard stopped, "A fool's room," he said to Makail, while letting go with one hand to unlock the cage. Once the cage opened, he untied Makail's arms and propelled him into his new dwelling.

Alone

    Makail walked slowly toward the wall opposite the bars. Centered at the very top of this wall, he noticed a small opening to the outside. Even though the slit hardly gave enough room for his fingers to slip through, he reached his hand to the opening, feeling nature's warmth, as spring brought great heat to the queen's territory. With his left hand, he reached to the side wall farthest away from the other chambers, opposite the wall where a kush waited for his rest. Man had not constructed this wall, for nature's burst derived the mountain on which this castle ends. Makail knew he dwelled in the chamber farthest to the north. Recalling the view from his stagger to the chamber doors, that immense balcony, likely for the queen, must hover directly above him. But the queen headed toward Pithlyn's gates, leaving her mass for any number of sundowns.

As the queen approached the gates, Fidelis caught up to her. Before entering the gates, he held the handle of Makail's sword toward her, holding the encased blade, and said, "This would be better kept in your carriage. We do not want the patrons of Favally to feel as though we come with a threat." She nodded her head and grasped the handle of the sword, bringing it into her sphere, as Fidelis strode to the front. She gazed at the handle with its beautiful decorations, so well crafted, so familiar. She slipped the blade from the case for examination. A few chinks on its surface, but the edge had no marks and could slice a tender touch, as she rubbed her finger along the blade, checking the sharpness. Yes, she knew this blade, for it had once belonged to a great protector of Pithlyn past, and it could sliver skin with gentle grazes. She recased the blade, hiding it behind her under a pile of fresh garments.

The connecting land from Pithlyn to Favally was the shortest distance between two masses in the entire sphere. Thus leaving soon after dawn would have them to the third village within Favally just before dusk. The terrain along the pass held fairly constant, relatively flat, and low to the water wielding on either side, although the width of this land carried more thickness than the length. Anyone utilizing the pass could smell the season in the air, whether traveling during the coldest days or warmest days. Nothing interrupted the scent of the season. To travel from Pithlyn to Favally presented a pleasant day without a reason for fear or sadness. Queen Bidellia planned on using the day's journey to relax and mentally reiterate the purpose of this adventure: to seek what Pithlyn can't provide for her. Instead, she thought of how it takes great courage, or much ignorance, to prevent the progress of the royal party's endeavor. The man who had attempted to do so earlier in the day, Makail, appeared to possess more of a courageous air than an ignorant air. His stature, physique, and grit appeared great enough to fight off her accompanying nobleman, yet he allowed Fidelis to take him away, as she'd instructed. The man was bold enough to stand before her and respectful enough to adhere to her request. If the man had not been of Dymetrice, she could have seen him as an admirable opportunity for love.

In his chamber, Makail lay on the kush quietly, repeating the thoughts of his predicament. Overcome by nympholeptic feelings, he sprung his torso upright and mumbled, "At once, I hear the voices of my past. My parents said this queen will keep me safe, yet she confines me to this wretched hole," he rose to his feet as his voice gradually revealed more force, "surrounding me with wretched souls of men, and only for innate Dymetrice roots. This Queen Bidellia, the immortal queen, who thrust this filth on me, a loathsome rule, may never understand the strength I hold, and my protection spans to boundless spans, yet she deduces me to sleep with rats when I could bring her glory's greatest gift."

The guards overheard the ranting, and one said wearily, "Close it, Fifteen."

Makail carried on, not hearing the guard at all, "So why'd she throw me to this tiny cell without a chance to prove goodwill to her? For I have come to seek the ways of life on Pithlyn Mass, a mass my soul has felt to be my destined home, rejoice, and grace. I've come to Pithlyn not to cause ado but put to rest the unrests of the past."

The same guard looked to his fellow men, and said "Do you hear fifteen? He's talking nonsense about who knows what." The other three guards didn't acknowledge him much, slightly nodding their heads while reading notes from the queen and itinerary from the head guard. "Strange."

Makail never fluttered in his words. He spoke as boldly as ever now, pacing across his room from front to back. "Oh, Queen Bidellia never gave a chance, and since she's summoned someone such a scorn, I'm left to dwell in dwellings all alone, so now my rage is for the queen's return, or once again, how could she keep me safe?" his boldness dashed by perplexity, wondering aloud. "Immortal queen, my parents' last request. A lovely queen, heartbreaking queen, indeed. A kind and loving queen to meet this eye." He closed his eyes, stopping the pace as he faced the back wall. "When wrath subsides and I can find my head, it may be true that I'm in love," shaking his head, he still hadn't opened his eyes. He rubbed his index finger and thumb over his eyes, before tilting to the opening in the wall. He let out a deep sigh, uttering, "Makail."

The clanking of a sword on the bars startled him back to reality. He twirled around quickly to see who bothered. A guard stood there snarling, "Are we going to have a problem with you, Fifteen?"

"No sir," Makail replied calmly. "I've got it figured out now. No troubles."

"What is your findings," the guard asked curiously.

"I have found my purpose."

"Good," the guard said, understanding the process of repentance. In Pithlyn, one who is sentenced to the High Confinary must first know what they've done wrong; second, understand a form of life to prohibit the possibility of repeating the wrong; third, take ownership of a newfound purpose; and fourth, portray adherence to the new purpose. "But you have just arrived. It will take much more than a simple sentence for us to grant your freedom. It is the queen's order, and it is her word to allow you out."

"Then I await the queen," he said with a sly smile. As the guard walked away annoyed, Makail flopped on the kush, satisfying himself with thoughts of this new home until Bidellia returns to her castle. With that realization, he comforted himself and drifted to a slumber in the middle of the morning.

Queen Bidellia and Fidelis pleasantly made it past Pithlyn Pass before the sun took aim at the horizon in front of them. As they progressed through the first couple villages, Fidelis did all the talking, only peeking back to Bidellia, checking if her face revealed any such interest. With each of the first authoritators shuttering in their words toward her, she knew neither would be right for her. If the village authoritator hadn't the courage to speak proudly and fearlessly to her, none of those within would either, such a rule by which they proceeded without viewing all a village had to offer. In Trilox, the two received more of the same from the authoritator, even though he'd expected the appearance. His utterances showed that he'd been toiling for the past days on how to act when the two enter his village. He stammered on every word as he introduced them to the finest lodging the village could offer: the authoritator's residence with two separate rooms with beds, another room to prepare meals and eat, and a fourth room with a large table for committee meetings. The authoritator would sleep in the dwelling of a village committee member for the night. Eventually, Fidelis had enough with the man fumbling over his words and kindly said, "We shall find the night fine from here, thank you," inquiring him to leave.

The two mingered into the separate rooms to slip on fresh clothes for the night. After changing, Bidellia remained on the bed, considering her time away from Pithlyn in search of love. She wondered if she should have left her mass to find an eventual king for it. Certainly, whomever she deemed worthy would be equally respected, and he would have to prove his greatness to the people. Her primary concern lain in the fact that her love, her mass, should yield the one for her. However, the Goddess of Love could appoint Bidellia's one true love in the rarest of places during any time of the goddess's existence, knowing Bidellia would find him, and right now, Bidellia could sense the imminence of his presence. Unlike three hundred years ago, her senses felt something real, something alive. Her long life's true love existed now, in the present. She shook her head in confusion, standing from her night's bed, wishing the goddess could just plop her love right in front of her instead feeling obliged to search the faraway lands.

She walked to the kitchen area where Fidelis had discovered a few indulgences for the two to enjoy. On the table, he'd placed fresh berries, crispies—which were airy puffs of sweet bread—and cocoa-powdered wafers. Bidellia raised her eyebrows with a nod of her head, impressed. She took a seat and began picking at the berries when Fidelis began: "You've been incredibly quiet today, my queen. Is there a bother of yours?"

Shrugging her shoulders, she shook her head while plopping the first berry in her mouth. Letting out a sigh, she turned her head toward her night's room, confessing, "Lone soul I am," she touched the back of her ear with her left index finger then finished, "with most of man so meek."

"Now, now, my queen, with your reputation, it will be difficult for any man to approach you outside the castle walls without a sense of inferiority. You have captured the souls of every Pithlyn person, and those of Favally have the same respect for you. Those of Indiffrin do not differ from these feelings. Residents of Glaci hold a heightened respect for you as well, whether they are man or gargentwan. This hunt may have no end." He stared at Bidellia who offered nothing but hope escaping her eye. "Dymetrice and Zyder are the two masses who have not fully come to terms with you, but I'm afraid their reaction to you would be unfavorable at best."

As the words left his mouth, Bidellia's mind retreated to a vision of Makail from Dymetrice, but she quickly winced her eyes to oust the image. "Dymetrice, cold and dark without a soul, or not a kinder soul extending care, and Zyder differs none, accepting dole and praising high before Dymetrice air."

"I understand such concerns, my queen," they both continued nibbling, "and I would far from ever recommend you run this trial through those territories. I do, though, want to express my feelings on this journey. I pray you do find the one who is right for you. It is the sole reason we've embarked on this effort. However, this is no easy task. To find a man brash enough to stand before the living goddess queen and ask for her hand? Not even I have such audacity."

"But Favally," she began hesitantly, "should have the one who's right." Taking a very deep sigh, she tilted her head toward the ceiling, exhaling, "Oh, now the surest queen is left unsure."

"Yes," Fidelis replied, "it will be best for us to rest now. When the sun wakes us, we will continue. I will clean the table, and you should try to rest." As Bidellia rose from her seat to head for the bed she'd occupy that night, Fidelis left her with, "Let us hope for better direction from the gods tomorrow."

Nodding her head in agreement, she walked through the door leading to her bed, where she said quietly with a tone of dejection, "I know I'll sleep alone again tonight."

Alone

She cuddled tightly in her bed, as she always had, to fall asleep in the tight grip of the surrounding blankets.

Scattered Stars

On the prison floor of the Pithlyn Palace, Makail had woken up to the guards yelling, "Dinner!" As Makail blinked his eyes awake, his soul emptied, remembering those guards had thrust him into this chamber, and he must exude his best behavior until his chance to gain the queen's attention pranced before him. How long would he have to suffer for no wrong doing, he wondered when a guard unlocked the bolt that had trapped Makail in the chamber. The guard held the door wide, and Makail asked, "Are you letting me leave?"

"Ha," the guard hissed, "only to have a bite of what the rest of this castle could not finish. Now get in line!"

Makail followed the orders, walking to the back of the line that filed to two tables—once occupied by the four guards—filled with scraps of food. All twelve of the other prisoners stood in the line ahead of him. A few piled the scraps on the wooden plates while the others waited eagerly. Makail, however, waited quietly, unfamiliar with the atmosphere and order. Those who'd earned more seniority in the confinary dished themselves first, which gave reason to Makail standing in the back of the line.

The man in front of Makail turned around to face him with eyes as dark brown as his skin. "The line goes slow, but we'll get our food. My name is Cil. They brought me here yesterday."

"Thanks. My name is Makail. They brought me here on today's morning."

"I know. I watched them bring you in, and then I heard you rambling something. What was that about?"

"What goes on here?" Makail asked, disregarding the question.

"What do you mean?"

"Do we simply sit on our kush all day, waiting for them to let us eat?"

"Only on your first day," Cil responded. "Coming in at night shortened my first day, but today after lunch we had to pull small unwanted plants from the steps out front. I suppose they give us small jobs every day, and if anybody disobeys, then they disobey the Queen of Pithlyn, which you never want to do. She'll thrash down an even harsher punishment, like sending somebody out on a boat to find his own way, or throwing him in that chamber across from yours."

Cil had reached the front of the table; grabbing a plate, he began scooping the remaining food and Makail followed, continuing the conversation, "There is no chamber across from mine."

"It is the wall you see. You'll see the door as you walk back to your room. When that door is closed, no light can enter. To keep such a prisoner alive, the guards throw food through a one-way clap door at the top. The person must stay in there for five sundowns, unless he proves stubborn—then he has to remain for five more."

"How do you know all this if you only arrived yesterday?"

"Have you noticed I talk a lot?"

With tight lips, Makail raised his head slowly before dropping his chin down, realizing his answer. "So if I prefer not to talk to anybody, I should avoid you?"

"Yes," Cil replied easily. "Then we pester you all day because you think you're better than us. Talk with me, we can be the new guys together, which is less complicated than being the new guy alone, especially out doing those jobs every day."

"Must be what they meant by suffering in here," Makail joked.

All thirteen men stood between the tables and the

wall of cells, eating off the wooden plates with their bare hands. All of them spoke within groups, as if a few small cliques had formed. Makail mainly observed, listening to Cil describe each person as he knew them. The three with the most seniority huddled together: Hanz, followed by Grudon and Wulym. Wulym's stature surpassed that of everybody else, and his arms hoarded more strength than the rest. The other two appeared as children standing next to him. Suddenly, Hanz noticed the new guy in the confinary, "You, what's your name?"

After Cil nudged his arm, Makail stated his name. Wulym intruded on the conversation, explaining to Hanz, "He's the batty bugger who ranted on when he arrived. He thinks he's in love." Hanz, Grudon, and Wulym roared laughing after the comment.

"You've mistaken my words, words meant not for such ears," Makail refuted, beginning to feel heat rising through his shoulders.

Through his snickering, Hanz barked, "Then next time keep your words quieter to not have them miss taken."

"Next time," Makail began, "keep your ears from my words."

Cil watched, impressed by the calm confidence Makail expressed with his tone as he spoke back to the three. Nobody comes into the confinary and talks to those with seniority like that. Cil stared at him with his lips apart, wondering what in this sphere he could have been thinking. As Cil expected, Hanz came back with another, "Next time you disrespect me, I'll make it well worth my five days of darkness."

"Unless I'm the one to spend the days in there," Makail undercut his words.

"You won't," Wulym deeply interfered.

Cil immediately put his hand to Makail's chest, "Calm, Makail, calm." Seeing Cil impede, the three reverted to their own conversation.

"Indeed, I'm very calm. They're not worthy of worry. This is good meal, even if it is scraps from above. Grilk is my favorite."

"Yes, the most plentiful animal in all of Pithlyn."

"Really?" Makail speculated.

"Certainly. Everybody in Pithlyn knows that. Are you not form here?" Cil inquired.

"I am of Dymetrice. I've traveled here seeking the queen's attention, only to have her shun me."

"So that's why you're here," said Cil, wide eyed. Pithlyn allowed no uninvited Dymetrice man to pass through the gates. Makail posed as an intruder on the highest level.

The night passed quietly. Bidellia slept tightly furled in the Trilox Authoritator's bed with Fidelis soundly sleeping in the other room. And as the sun began its daily climb, a diaphanous green beamed through stained glass windows, shining across the sheets and through her softly awakening face, sending such a green mist to her blondest hair. She tossed her body, giving her back to the window as a smile crept to her face. Bidellia's mind danced a remarkable dream last night, "She speaks: 'the perfect man survives for her,'" she remembered with a blanket covering half her mouth. In her dream, the Goddess of Love had spoken to Omnerce. Bidellia often dreams of the gods speaking to each other or to her. When these dreams occur, they speak truth because of Bidellia's status as the Living Goddess of Prodigion. Having twirled through this dream, her entire soul believed this journey would result in success, and excitement thrilled her skin this morning.

She quietly changed from her sleeping gown to her royal attire in a state of pure satori. She thought she would have heard Fidelis fiddling in the next room by now, but tranquility filled the entire dwelling. Inquisitively, she slipped through her door and headed toward the other room. Tapping on his door, she nudged it open only to find her trusted advisor zonked in a deep blink. She playfully rolled her eyes, shaking her head with half a smile. The queen walked softly to the bedside, listening to his soft snore. While standing next to Fidelis, she quickly grabbed the sheet covering him and swooped it off him. He jerked his body upright and swung his legs to the floor. "Oh, my queen! You shouldn't startle me like that!"

She grinned widely, nodding her head satisfied with her small prank. Becoming serious with the same easy expression, she said, "He lives today, so let us search and find."

"Yes, that is the meaning of all this. I will be ready promptly, and we shall travel farther into Favally today. If he is out there, as you believe, we will find him soon enough."

"And find we shall," she said pleasantly. "He walks the present soil."

As the queen left, Fidelis hurried to dress himself, fumbling through his royal attire, and rushing to prepare the raxars for another day's journey, which would be only the second of many with the extent of Bidellia's intense search through Favally. Fidelis never overslept the way he had this morning, and he attempted to relinquish his fault with blundered morning haste. In as short a time as possible, he had the queen in her royal coach ready to leave Trilox. The authoritator had waited patiently for them to see if they had a nice night and if there would be anything else he could do to help them. Fidelis rejected the latter offer after thanking him for the quarters.

One strand of mountains linked across Favally, but they rested west of everything the two would see for several days, and only a few villages worked west of the mountains. For the day's journey, four villages separated Trilox from King Briley's castle. They made swift stops through each village, as Fidelis verbalized everything. All authoritators acted like most, unable to act or speak with their normal utterance; all of them quivered in her presence. Nothing ignited the queen's curiosity enough to spur words, until reaching the castle.

King Briley personally greeted the two at his door, welcoming them to his mass. Following his lead into the castle, they walked through a square room with a white floor, white walls higher than the fifteen-foot doors opening his castle, and green doors. There were three doors on the wall in front of them and one door on each of the side walls. Briley led them to the right door of the wall opposite their entrance, which exposed a short, flame-lit brick hallway, which, aside from the torches scent, smelled as though old water had just been cleaned away. Behind the next door, a long open table with a white table cloth centered in the room and pictures of past kings hung along the brick walls. King Briley walked to the opposite end of the table to sit in the largest chair over-fluffed with green fur. Fidelis and Bidellia had split sides of the table to end up sitting across from each other.

"I understand you've come to my land believing a man exists to spend all of time with you, and he may be of Favallian blood."

Even though his face had cocked toward Bidellia during his statement, Fidelis felt obliged to respond. "Yes, she has noticed that all men in Pithlyn understand her power as the immortal queen and Living Goddess, so they treat her as such, baffled at the sight of her, stammering through words. She believes she can find a good man here in Favally who will not look at her in a palpitatingly glorified light."

"It's quite a quest you have, my queen," Briley began. "A rare man you seek, and I would have my doubts that you would find any man on Prodigion worthy of your ever presence." His eyes jumped to the ceiling before refocusing on the queen. "It would be like having your father line up all his stars in perfect order to have the right man come leaping to you from star to star."

"Then soon enough, the stars shall shine aligned," the queen offered.

At the end of her words, three castle servants came into the room with dinner plates for each of them. Unleavened bread, steaming vegetables, syrupy fruit medley, and a hunk of white meat from a hen filled their plates and nostrils. The queen ate quietly while Fidelis and Briley carried on about their travels so far, Pithlyn's current state of peace, and the queen's sudden impulse to set a man beside her upon the highest throne on Prodigion.

As the three finished their meals, the queen heard them describing the utter difficulty of her endeavor, and she interjected, "To find him, we must rest to bear our moil."

Fidelis rose, "She's right. we should be heading to a visitor's room."

"Oh, the grand visitor's room for the two of you!" King Briley responded.

The three walked back through the musky hallway to the square entry room. King Briley led them through the far left door on that wall opposite the castle's main doors. After rising up two flights of white cement stairs with green railing and surrounded by white walls, they walked all the way to the end of a green carpeted white hallway, passing numerous green doors. A couple doors tilted ajar, and Fidelis saw what appeared to be guards inside the rooms. Inside the door at the end of the hallway, the grand guest room awaited Pithlyn royalty. King Briley opened the door, and two massive beds lain side by side with six feet of carpet separating them. A stand for books and possessions stood against the wall between the beds. A table surrounded by three heavily cushioned benches took up the left side of the room while a table for meals and conversation held on the opposite side of the room. It smelled like a fresh spring morning, and looked cozy enough for a queen's liking.

King Briley saw that the two would become comfortable within the room and left. Fidelis went off to a side room behind the meal table where the walls would hide him to undress and redress into sleepwear. Queen Bidellia did the same, and acknowledged it safe for Fidelis to come out once she had on her evening gown, saying, "I'm set."

Fidelis walked to his bed and pulled the blankets over his body, as Queen Bidellia had already done in her own bed. "Seven villages past, five more tomorrow. We may hope one of them has that right kind of man you seek. If they don't, we will continue with more villages until we find where your fellow gods have hidden him."

"Despite our lack of luck so far, he's there; he's here; the gods have seen my star."

Empty Days

After breakfast, guards led illmates out the hatch door to begin their duties. Six guards escorted the thirteen men from the confinary. One guard walked in front of the prisoners, one trailed on a raxar with a trailer full of tools attached, and two staggered on each side of the single-file line. Each guard held a long torch, which doubled as a walking stick, in one hand and a shoker, a black metal rod—narrowing to a point opposite the handle—in the other hand. The prisoners, like the meal line, proceeded in order based on seniority, all wearing only loose black pants halfway down their shins. If any of the men spoke a word, the nearest guard would nudge him with his shoker. The warm air, interrupted by soft cool breaths, filled the fresh season's atmosphere, which held the scent of an early spring morning. The bright sun blitzed through the blue sky, striking the mountain walls with a furious glow. Sporadic trees awoke, glittered with buds ready to burst into leaves.

The guards led the men to the base of a nearby mountain where a bolted secret tunnel allowed for entry. If men passed this wall, they would not recognize a door, for the coloring of the door, powdered with mountain dust, allowed for it to camouflage against the surroundings. A flap of land could be gently lifted to reveal the doors lock, and only the guards had the proper tools to open this door. When the crew reached this mountain side, each man was directed to turn his head in the opposite direction, simply for the guards' reassurance.

The man-chiseled and -dug tunnel opened tall enough for any man to walk through with ease, as it sloped downward quickly; however, due to a lower clearance, the trailing guard dismounted his raxar and secured him in place on a hook carved into the mountain wall. The steep decline continued as they frequently passed openings to other tunnels on the right and left. Makail and Cil had no idea where the line would eventually lead, but the rest of the prisoners had done this before. As the dark air chilled, Makail and Cil straggled behind the rest of the line, doing everything not to earn a nudge from the guards. One nudge and either would end up as the most closely watched prisoner for several days—until proven compliant.

At the base of the long slope, some men revealed weariness in expression while others searched the grotto lit only by the glow of six torches. The base, a relatively small, circular platform, led into seven more channels. Half boulders protruded from overhead, as if threatening to collapse on the party. The leading guard paused only momentarily, before heading to the third opening from the left. Makail, as the line's last man, never had the opportunity to fully view the corridor, as the entire line followed through the area too quickly.

Moments after everybody had entered through the directed path, a voice echoed through the barrage, as the lead guard announced, "For hundreds of years, men under Queen Bidellia have come through these paths to carve the walls in search of the gold sheathed within them. Today you will scratch through more rock to fill your dishes with gold, and nobody will leave until each man's dish is full and inspected. You will begin on my word!"

The row persisted for many strides before the leading guard shouted for them to halt. The guards supplied each prisoner with the same tool, which had a wooden handle and a thin black metal spike, as well as a round dish, dropping in the center like a cone with a one-inch diameter bottom, holding the equivalence of two one-gallon milk jugs. Once all prisoners had what they needed to mine gold, the leading guard hollered for them to begin. The men separated from the line, some going left others to the right. While it may seem odd for prisoners to be involved with such a task due to untrustworthiness, in no way could any of them actually obtain shavings of gold for themselves. Even if an attempt were made to collect for own self, they would get caught and spend five days in the obscurium. Each prisoner hacked at the stone wall with the flames' flickering glimmer as his only light, and chatter began to arise, which the guards allowed to a degree. No guard would stand for an overhaul of clamor, as one stood on each end of the drudging men, while four paced down the middle.

Wulym, who'd begun his work toward the leading guard, worked his way back toward the trailing guard, claiming his spots had been clear of gold. None of the other prisoners paid him much attention since his impatience typically carried him to act irrationally. His constant movement during grudge duties had become the norm. With so far an empty dish, he found a spot on the opposite side of Makail, stating, "Lots of gold here! I can smell it."

Makail's eyes glared to their corners and bounced back to the wall. He said nothing in response, just kept grating the stone for gold. Men had scraped through these underground alleys for hundreds of years. Each different trail symbolized another crews venture. Every trail had gold encased in the walls. Mixed with the stone underground, gold swam everywhere. Every time man entered, he'd come out with as much gold as he could bear to work for, which is why the royal committee knew great security measures needed to be taken in order to protect all the gold. For the same reason, Wulym's cry for no gold in his area could not have been more than a sham.

"Queen Bidellia," Wulym said, followed by a steady, elongated "m" sound. Sensing the mockery in Wulym's voice, Makail discerned antagonism but remained silent.

Several moments past with Wulym in silence, chipping away, beginning fill his dish. With his tool scratching the wall, he repeated himself.

Makail, staring at the wall, replied, "Since you've been standing there, I've wondered two things I never thought I'd ever care about: One, what kind of odor does gold possess; and two, what is it with you and the words Queen Bidellia?"

"Gold smells like your mouth after I stuff this dish down your throat, and I'm in love with Queen Bidellia," followed by an uproarious laughter, which evoked the end guard to order silence.

Makail knew the problem, linking it back to the conversation during yesterday's evening meal. He ignored the threat and quietly responded, "Did you have trouble sleeping last night after our conversation?"

"Lose sleep over a fool who thinks he could be in love with the Living Goddess? I would never!"

By now, Makail's dish already neared the brim, as he used his skill to trickle a few meaningless pebbles away from the sought gold. Wulym's held the opposite amount, appearing to have just begun, even though he chiseled through the stone with complete ease and should have finished first. With his focus more on annoying Makail, the hard-rock gold mining became second priority. Wulym knew from experience, even if he made a late start, the rest of the crew would not wait on him.

Wulym continued, "What would ever cause you to believe Queen Bidellia would love rubble like you."

Offended, he stepped away from his spot while Wulym watched him leave. Makail walked to the end guard, handing him the dish of gold, "This is finished and ready for inspection." He began back to his place of mining with his inner rage no longer in hiding. He stopped behind Wulym who could sense his presence, peaking over his shoulder. As Makail caught his eye, he shoved his palm into Wulym's back, lifting him a few feet in the air, slamming him against the wall, which was less than arm's length from him. "Don't ever speak in arrogance of another man's sacred endeavor!"

The guard's couldn't react to the thump, as one

inspected Makail's dish, the two nearest had passed their spots, and the two farthest checked the immediate miners. Wulym could react. His face had smashed into the stone hard enough to bloody his nose and send cobwebs through his head. Due to the verticality of the shove, Wulym flopped to the ground on his back as his gold spilled with him. Yet, he shook off the blow. Slowly climbing to his feet, he breathed, "Fool," flinging his fist to meet Makail's cheek.

On contact, Makail shouted a groan for the guards to hear, as he fell to the ground. Wulym retrieved his dish then lurched toward Makail, thrusting his right knee on his stomach, applying as much pressure as he could. He dug gold from the dish and tried stuffing it in Makail's mouth, forcing his hand through his lips, saying "I'll stuff this right down your throat, you fool."

Two guards rushed and pulled Wulym off Makail. Before Makail could rise, Wulym—who had both his arms twined with the guards—jerked a leg out, striking Makail in the side. The guards vehemently escorted Wulym to the end beyond where he had begun the day, exclaiming, "When we get back, you won't be seeing the sun for a long time."

As each man finished, they all had to wait patiently for others to complete the task. Wulym finished last as his pace declined after the scuffle, losing enthusiasm and interest. Nonetheless, he did fill the dish, and everybody formed the same line used earlier in the day. Even Wulym took his place as third in line. As much as the trek earlier declined, the trek back inclined. None of them had the energy to make it all the way back to the surface. But they toughed it out, making it on their final dig of the muscles. The walk from the mountain entrance to the prison entrance bared less strain, more relaxing after the difficulty of the underground hike.

As prisoners filed into the room of chambers, two guards clinched Wulym and threw him into the obfuscation while the others began to form a line for the late lunch. Waiting in line, Cil turned to Makail, examining his puffy left cheek. "He really set a hard hit on you, didn't he?"

"Yes," Makail responded, "but at least I'm not in there," pointing his thumb over his right shoulder.

"You don't think you could defeat him outside of this supervision, do you?"

"Let's just stay at, I did not want to live in that chamber. Besides, outside of these walls, I would hold my sword during a duel. His strength lasts no chance to my skill."

This remark of his swordsmanship was the only words he ever spoke of his gifts while locked in the confinary. He never led anyone to believe he could crumble mountains or blaze flames or run faster than the sun's light shines to the sphere. He sat quietly for twenty-four more sunrises, humming himself to sleep after performing the duties of the castle, which changed from day to day, but Makail noticed every nine days, the duties repeated: gold mining; hunt for food; clean the guards' rooms; clean the committee members' quarters; clean the throne room; hunt for food; miscellaneous task, involving an urgent need within the castle; clean clothes of guards and committee members; and work on the outside of the castle, such as the steps. He pleasantly obeyed instructions and continued to reveal his repentance with hopes of an early exit; since Queen Bidellia personally directed his sentence, however, he needed to wait for her approval before release. Primarily, Cil remained as the only one with whom Makail spoke, though he refused to develop too much of a friendship with him. Makail had come to Pithlyn with one purpose, and he would have nothing distract from his guidance.

Wulym had come from the bleakest after five days, but he ended any feuding with Makail. They never shook hands or anything, but they kept their distance. Five days is long enough to consider somebody's strength of pushing a man of Wulym's stature into the wall with such force only using one hand. Mind boggling, really, and Wulym realized it best to not pursue antagonism on

Chapter 11

Makail.

Tranquility had filled the breezes carrying from shore to shore during Queen Bidellia's absence. Not a village in her land found urgent issues requiring her prompt attention, and each mass held within domains. For the past two hundred years, little rumbling had ever quaked between any two masses. Considering three villages' issues had recently found resolutions at her appointment, the queen had felt comfortable leaving her land for an extended period. Thus, her spontaneous excursion to Favally had come with impeccable timing.

In Favally, the queen had troubles still. No man stood bold enough to rise with grit, for each had acted as they always will. This showed her soul a need to quickly quit, and yet, her journey formed a long retreat with gawking men who stare and shy away then kiss the footprints of her stepping feet. Thus, on a day when skies began to gray, she told Fidelis time had come to leave. Dejected, Queen Bidellia searched above, and leaving, wondered who the gods believe to be the one surviving as her love. An empty journey ended all for naught; arriving home, she lingered deep in thought.

The Duel

Another long but enjoyable day of hunting had concluded for illmates. On such days, each prisoner hauled wooden planks, which carried their hunting spears, to the hunting grounds with aspirations of hauling back a heap of successes. They traveled to the south and east from the castle where myriad animals ran free. A dense population of grilk lived in the area, as well as wild boar—oversized, aggressive pigs—coyogs, wild turkeys, along with smaller game, like tree climbers and grass bounders. The assignment commanded illmates to bring back at least one of the larger animals. Not one person could head for the castle unless each had fulfilled the assignment. Before night nestled, the last illmate punctured his prey, and the line of sun-exhausted men filed back to the chambers.

As the men approached Pithlyn Palace, before

splashing through the shallow stream, Makail noticed several raxars departing from the steps' base. Nudging Cil's shoulder, he asked in a whisper, "Where are they going?" Part of him feared enemy raxars had arrived; another hoped for Cil's answer.

"Those are the queen's raxars," he remembered from the royal visit that convicted him of theft and perjury. "They take her wherever she needs to be, so she must have recently returned from her leave."

"So Queen Bidellia is in her castle?" Makail sought reassurance.

Sensing a child-like thrill, Cil said, "Yes, it appears the queen will rest in the queen's bed tonight," sounding like a mother speaking to her toddler.

Makail stared to his feet, grumbling within his breaths, growing overly anxious to sit in his chamber alone. He'd waited long enough for the queen's return, and now he fuddled himself, muddling over how he could snare the queen's attention for a moment to show her who he really was. He'd considered various options during his days in the chamber, like blazing past the guards and jumping to her balcony; or causing the mountain wall of his chamber to crumble just enough giving him adequate room for an escape; or creating a diversion by expanding flames of torches in the dungeon so he could slip outside unnoticed. He concluded to not use any of his premeditated strategies because each required the use of his skills, and he desired to obtain Bidellia's attention naturally.

After the social time that immediately followed dinner, all illmates dispersed to their individual chambers to rest for the night. Makail's heart beat nauseatingly loud, as he sat on his kush, and the guards made a round to check places and lock every chamber gate. He knew Queen Bidellia stood directly above him. He could feel her near existence, for he'd never felt such a numbing feeling overwhelm his every sense. Nothing sounded different or appeared different from the previous nights, but everything felt different. He laid his head back to the edge of his kush with his feet aiming toward the locked gates of his cell. Closing his eyes, the melody of the capisongs began to flow from his soul through his lips.

In her sprilen, Queen Bidellia had not retired to her bed for the night. She sat at her desk reading through letters and notes of happenings during her time away. She had focused deeply on the concerns and elations of her people since she returned from her expedition. She hadn't thought once of the disappointment stemming from her empty journey until she looked into the dark sky beyond her balcony. Few stars shone toward her as she walked outside to fold her arms atop the waist-high rail, encircling the edge. She viewed above, dwelling deeply on her recent misfortunes. She called out, "Oh, gods above, reveal my man for life, for all I've faced have shriveled like a prune! My soul is sinking, swapping hope for strife." Softly in the background, her ears caught a harmonious and pure melody, as her words faded. Her head jerked from side to side, speculating the origins of the sound. With her eyes, she searched the caliginous foregrounds below her balcony; she searched the mountain wall immediately to her left; she searched her room behind her. Nothing moved or gave signs of life. That beautiful melody, though, grew boisterously in her ears. She had never heard such a pure pitch, so Bidellia knew her mind toyed not with her tonight. Like whisking, she pivoted. Her robust intuition told her from where the music hummed. She whipped through her room, snatching what she needed, before quickening her paces through the corridor.

Passing guards through the dark stairwell to the dungeon, they bowed, and her head nods acknowledged their respect. Reaching the bottom of these steps, she thrust open the doors with her knuckles, as she burst into the dungeon. Each of the four guards on night duty stood from their positions and lowered their chins. With a sword dangling from each of her hands, she said, "Now, show me to the man who hums the tune."

On her demand, other prisoners chattered in mockery

of Makail, provoking Queen Bidellia to retort, "And silence to the ones who wrongly shout!" At the same time, one guard said, "He is this way, my queen." He walked her toward the chambers where every prisoner behind their bars had risen to their feet, paying homage to the sphere's highest queen. The guard stopped in front of Makail's chamber, where he had ceased his sounds, now sitting upright on his kush. Queen Bidellia motioned for the guard to leave her side; despite his insistence on staying, her narrowing eyes and firm lips told him he'd been ordered to leave.

Her eyes tunneled to Makail, as he sat, staring at the floor. Never letting his silhouette escape her sight, she spoke, "My gods, this can't be who you've sent for me, for he's not rising to respect my clout."

Makail felt the burn of her glare on him. Burning hotter within were her words. "Respect." He uttered, shifting his eyes to Bidellia. Makail wanted desperately for the queen to see him as the man his parents raised a boy to become. But part of him resented her rash decree. He continued, "You slew me in this dirty cage, expecting me to show respect for one who's ordered me this filth for nothing wrong?" The volume of his voice increased, "You've put me here! Disgusting stench and pests and neighbors who annoy me to the gods. Respect! I cannot give respect to one who cannot give to me the honor of a chance to gain, or even lose, respect." He stood from his kush and walked to the bars, grabbing a hold of them with each hand. In a whisper, he finished, "And yet my soul desires you, evermore."

In more than three hundred years, no man had ever spoken an intimate word to her. She broke back one step, wide-eyed with quick tremors from her wrist through the fingertips. Despite a disbelieving open mouth, she kept calm, knowing she must act as though the words had never resounded. Straightening her lips, the queen used the tip of her sword to unlatch Makail's secured door and slide it open. Subduedly, the queen requested her intent, "Perhaps a duel proves that petty plea," referring to Makail's claim of doing nothing wrong.

Makail hesitated before stepping into the narrow half hallway beside Bidellia where she handed him his own sword with the point directed toward the ground. As he gripped the handle, he said, "I've missed this blade from which I've never strayed. With this," he looked to Bidellia, "I find my ease and greatest strength."

She glanced from his eyes to his hair to his feet and back to his eyes before cocking her head forward to lead him from the confinary, saying "Then we shall clash our swords at mountain's base." She led him past the silently standing guards, through the stairwell, and into the throne room where Makail slowed his pace, swirling his head, amazed by the size and beauty of it with several flames aglow to illuminate the walls and the queen's chair. While fascinated by the dim brilliance, Bidellia had made it to the front doors of her castle. Unlike during daylight, the only guards after dusk protected from the outside. When the queen wished leave during the night, she had to knock on the door a certain way. With a loose fist, she raised her right arm, tapping her wrist against the door then rolling her hand to her mid-finger knuckles to immediately cause a second tap. She repeated this quickly four more times. Hearing the consistent persistent thudding, Makail refocused and trotted to Bidellia as the doors began to open. The sheer height of these doors stunned him. He'd noticed the doors from afar, but they exuded a different profoundness when standing immediately before them, especially while cracking open ever so slowly.

After checking for Makail's presence behind her, Queen Bidellia dashed down the steps. Noticing her haste, Makail matched her step for step. The entire decline, Makail couldn't figure out what a sword fight with her would prove. He felt the need to act politely toward her after expressing his heavier-hearted feelings, but she demanded a sword fight.

She set foot on the quaint open plain that swallowed the final step; Makail immediately followed. Queen

Chapter 12

Bidellia took her place anticipating Makail to line up accordingly. He complied. With his arms folded, his sword dangled in his right hand, which was tucked inside his left elbow. He stood defiantly, body languaging that he wanted no part of a duel with this queen. Not that he didn't feel confident in his abilities, but how could he fight the most respected being on the sphere?

"We make our start," she snarled, wearing her warrior expression, "to see the swiftest scud." With her final word, she sprung toward Makail with her blade aimed below his folded arms, knowing if he actually came from the former protector of Pithlyn, his capabilities with a sword exceeded her own. But Makail did not react. He stood completely still until her blade came tearing at him inches from his stomach when he swirled his sword all the way around to undercut her blade away from contact. She kept her grip on the handle, and brought her sword back, readying for another jab while Makail remained motionless. She brought the sword to her left shoulder then swept it through the air, attempting to cut Makail's right side, but he swiveled the sword too swiftly and blocked again. The queen became fierce, eyes turning to ice, and the face of a warrior turned demonesque. Now her swipes came repeatedly and furiously. She stabbed high, low, center, left, right, leg sweep, center, right, high, left, low, center; and Makail clanked his sword against hers every time without breaking a sweat.

"Hold nothing back, for nothing scathes this face!" demanding an honest effort from Makail, wanting to see if Jivin's ineffable powers existed within him.

They stood two arm lengths apart, and Makail responded, "The problem there, my gifts will frighten you."

She winced her eyes back at him, challenging him to prove it. Effortlessly, he jumped over her, sliding his sword a fingernail from her nose as he passed her, eventually landing high on the mountain wall behind her. She whipped her body around to see him speeding toward her faster than anything the sphere had ever seen. As he gusted past her side, he used the flat of his sword to turn her body in the direction he headed so she could watch him zoom up the mountain on the other side of the open plain where he switched direction to press back toward her. Observing his Jivin-like speed, he charged directly at her, springing into the air. His legs appeared as if they'd frozen in mid-run; his outstretched left arm ended with his hand as his scope; his right arm angled back with his sword poised for the kill, aimed precisely to the queen's forehead. Just as he neared his strike, he pulled his position into a dive, right over her head, landing with his fists, and somersaulting to a halt. He quickly rose and stood immediately behind Bidellia with his sword at a diagonal across his body. Her back remained his only view when he stated, "Against the common man, he's finished now."

She rotated her position to face Makail. Her nose inches from his lips, she stepped back. Her eyes had become the kind and genuinely beautiful eyes Makail remembered from so many days ago. Her face had reverted to the friendly leader. Looking above, she said, "If only he were not Dymetrice blood."

At her words, Makail felt great disdain. "Dymetrice Mass once may have held my birth, but never will it hold my blood within."

Sensing his irritability, she calmly, said "At ease."

"I'd like a meaning of your ridicule," he begged.

With only a foot of air between the two, she pondered his inquisition. A void remained in her life after her adventure to Favally and her great dislike for the rulers and philosophies of Dymetrice past and present, yet here stood a man in front of her from Dymetrice not afraid of her, not timid, but bold and charged. She whispered "I may forever be forlorn."

"You think my blood and soul has come from there, but rest assured, the gods believe my soul belongs to Pithlyn, proving this..." his words dropped off as he thought of a way to prove his soul's home differed from his birthplace. He knew the difficulty in such a task, but then, while searching beneath the horizons, he thought of something. "Unless," he uttered as he walked past the queen.

"Unless…" she questioned.

"If you can follow me, I'll show you proof," he said confidently. He traipsed through the shallow stream with Bidellia shortly behind. Only a few strides after dampening their feet, Makail stopped to look left and right, standing in the wide alley. He turned to her, and said, "The beauty that these flowers hold is vast, but deeper rests the truest of their worth."

Queen Bidellia followed his eyes and said quietly, "My love's in this," referring to the bed as a whole.

Just as the words left her mouth, Makail spun his sword and sliced his left side four times. In the midst of his appeared delusions, Bidellia demanded, "Dymetrice born!"

Makail never hesitated or showed concern; instead, he attempted to calm her in saying, "I understand these flowers mean to heal, but pedals only heal a Pithlyn man." He picked a flower on the edge of the alleyway. Even though it was a white flower, meant only to heal the deepest of wounds, he knew it would work like magic. Plucking the pedals, he one by one set them on his wound with Bidellia watching closely. Each pedal gripped to his skin like a leech, giving him a tingling comfort, like a soothing ointment to the skin. Once he fully covered every slash mark, he pressed his hand against his side, evenly across the wounds, then skimmed each away in one motion. His flesh had returned to its natural color, and Bidellia gasped in amazement, knowing all too well the purpose of the flowers: to keep her men strong and healthy.

"You see, my queen," Makail announced, "you really are my queen."

Beautiful

You're not an easy man for me to know," Queen Bidellia stated with a bewildered stare. The two sat side by side in the alley with their backs inches from the white flowers, facing south.

"There'd be no fun if any other way," he smirked.

She shook her head with a slight lip reach, "You're born Dymetrice, now you're Pithlyn's pick. You run much faster than the wind can blow; you're sword is graceful, moving all too quick; and then, you blare through air without a care. Now, what's a fuddled queen to make of this?"

"A fuddled queen can make what she may please," he said, intending to speak lightly. As Queen Bidellia remained expressionless, he interpreted her words, "I feel you're asking me to speak my grounds. You want to know from where I've come to you and why I move with skill like no one else?"

She quickly nodded her head, saying "Do speak the truth and tell why you are rare." She had to understand Makail, as he'd already impressed her in more ways than anybody else in her long life. Her feelings had already opened for this man, but nothing could happen unless the two could be perfect for each other. The only way to ever figure that out is to understand the other.

Makail explained, "In brief, my parents lived on Pithlyn soil. The gods had granted them uncommon gifts to help protect the Pithlyn plains and hills. Combined, they'd crumble mountains, wave the deep, ablaze a forest, tip the trees, outfight a legion, run and jump like nothing else, and scale to peaks of any mountain top, but when my mother knew I turned inside, she wanted all the feuding gone and done. So she, and with my father, found a home: Dymetrice, near the king to keep at peace with hopes to make as friends with those they'd doomed. It started with success, but others talked; the next in line as king, now King Avar, had known the former plot to raze the reign. His foremost task was ending both their lives. My parents came aware of this and sent me off to live in Quintix Valley's woods, as they complied with dreaded kingly rule. You see now, only cowards flee from death, and only cowards let their children die. That's why they sent me there to hone my skills until I grew in strength enough to find the highest queen to ever breathe this air; a mighty task, but I survived," he hesitated with his words, staring Bidellia in the eyes, "for you."

Her body repelled by inches, eyes widening with her sharp inhale. In an oneiric voice, she said, "And you survived for everlasting bliss."

"No, I survived for your protecting hands. But then, my parents never mentioned all the beauty you possess in face and soul. Now what's a fuddled man to make of this?"

"I ought to share with you some tales of past, but first, you must have more to share on things."

"I'm rather boring other than my past. I lasted fourteen years in Quintix Woods before the time had come to seek your hand. I lived and trained, preparing for our time. There's really nothing else to offer you."

"The humming tunes," she inquired curiously, "are those the spells you cast?"

"Oh, ha! The gods had never given gifts for us to cast a spell on any soul. The humming comes from Quintix Valley life. The capisongs—the long-necked creatures—hum, caressing young to sleep with soothing tunes. I heard the beauty, studied pitch, and sang, repeating it the best I could until I sounded all the same in tune with them." He hesitated for a moment, looking into Bidellia's soft eyes. "Since coming here, I've thought of words for you to match the flowing stream the humming makes. At yours, I'd like to share my words with you."

She granted Makail permission with a kind hand gesture. Makail coughed a bit, then hummed the tune several times while Bidellia listened, smiling. Both had shut their eyes, and without any warning, his voice turned to lyrics:

> *Oh when her beauty sees my eyes again,*
> *She'll wonder what she had been thinking then*
> *I'll sing this song so she can see my soul*
> *And how she's everything I would extol.*
> *Her beauty holds a grace to never fail.*
> *Who put those diamonds where her eyes should hail?*
> *Who struck her teeth with perfect pearls of white*
> *And matched a frame of lips of perfect sight?*
> *I'd love to take her hand and show her me*
> *While holding tight to let our souls go free.*
> *If she could see the man I am inside,*
> *Perhaps our lives could lastingly collide.*
> *Oh when her beauty sees my eyes again,*
> *She'll hear my soul and grieve her thoughts from*
> > *then.*

"And that's the end," he stated, as his eyes opened to the queen. "I hope my words have pleased."

She had opened her eyes after the second line of his song, stunned he would challenge her thoughts. As the words continued to flow from his mouth, her soul began to rise with disbelief. Everybody in all the land knew of her beauty and her power. They all knew of her obvious immaculate form so well that they assumed the queen had heard it far too many times. Therefore, nobody ever dared to mention her ever-graceful appearance, which meant, nobody complimented her looks to her face. To hear Makail sing so elegantly of her melted everything inside her. For the majority of his song, she could not breathe, taking in his feelings, his soul. By the end, gazing into his deep eyes, she replied, "The song was beautiful," pausing to look toward her feet then back to his eyes, "as he who sings."

He smiled wider than he had since his youth. He could feel his heart racing, hands trembling, unsure what to do next. With an unnoticeable quiver in his voice, he said, "I'm overjoyed by such response from you." He slid his hand across the grass, attempting to match hers. On contact, she slipped her hand away.

"You still have very much to prove, Makail," she said startled. Nobody had reached for her hand in hundreds of years. Regaining composure, watching Makail glumly breathe with eyes wandering to the southern horizon, she clinched his hand only to whisper, "but there's a chance that you're my storytale."

She had released from his hand, and he stood up. Searching for nothing straight ahead with Bidellia still sitting next to his feet, he countered, "By reign of Omnerce, what's a storytale?"

Bidellia rose with tenderly swift movements, meeting the muddy eyes of Makail. In a soft melodic voice, she described, "A storytale is more than stories told, but not a tale for others' disbelief. It's when a man or woman finds the gold within a soul to keep through time not brief." Pivoting, she headed toward her castle while Makail watched her walking away. Before the stream, she stopped. Without looking back, she finished, "In Pithlyn, every soul will cherish theirs." The shallow water absorbed her sloshing feet; the grass bowed beneath her fleeting feet; the stone steps proudly played their role in her ascent to the castle until the doors waited with open arms to capture her. Makail watched from his original position the entire time, not chasing her, not questioning her, but letting her go. She never looked back, not even to thank him for the beautiful lyrics, not to say goodnight, not to give him an option of where to sleep.

Recent Past

Makail watched the doors close behind Bidellia. His eyes slid shut, as he tilted his head to the sky. He'd just experienced the night he'd anticipated since embarking on his path toward Pithlyn. But she walked away. He never expected everything to end in such abruptness. Her departure left a clutter of emotions running through him. Excitement to have been given the opportunity to show Bidellia the man he is; curiosity in how she really feels toward him and if she wants to see him again; disappointment for how she pulled her hand away and also left abruptly; affection with his feelings growing greater each moment at her side.

Makail opened his eyes, twirling his head to explore the night. Surrounded by darkness, everything appeared as shadows. The towering mountains, Pithlyn Palace, trees to the east all appeared as silhouettes in the dim air.

Chapter 14

In the sky, only a few stars shone with a glowing moon hazed by scattered clouds. The air had cooled since the duel, yet still no breeze. In addition to the flowers' scent, remnants of Bidellia's aroma, like a spring shower, lingered through his nostrils, and he could taste her breath every time he inhaled.

Despite the dark, he noticed no guards coming to force him back to the cage. He felt free to do as he may wish for the night. Of course, if he could truly follow his wishes, he would have walked with Bidellia back to the castle. So why didn't he follow her? She never demanded him to stay or not follow. However, she had left just moments after expressing her desire for Makail to prove more to her, which Makail had taken as a close to the night, as if Queen Bidellia had seen and heard enough for one night. He felt insufficient enough to not follow the queen's effervescent presence after that occurred. Standing in the grassy alley, he could not figure out what she wanted him to prove.

In a blur, Makail sped to the mountain just north of Bidellia's balcony. He scaled the wall, seeking a ridge or cavern. He knew he didn't want to reach too high of a point on the mountain, for that would lead to a gelid night. Since cool temperatures set a chill at sea level, the freeze began less than halfway to the top. While quickly climbing and scaling, his hand clopped on a flat service, low enough to still see the immensity of the queen's balcony. As he peered to this brief stone plane, he saw an arching crevice, forming a hole filled by a nest—a gantor nest. His eyes enthusiastically widened, thinking this would be a perfect bed for one night. Pulling himself to his feet, he leaned over the brim, which came up to his chest, and found four green eggs the size of his stomach. While in awe by the sheer size of the eggs, he heard the squawking shriek of mom soaring back to her unborn babies. He turned to the diving mom and shoved his hands to the air as if he'd just been caught red-handed, while sliding to the opposite side of the nest from where mom enclosed. As the mightily powerful gantor landed and clinched her six gangly toes on the nest, she leaned across her eggs, gaping her black beak wide enough to clamp Makail, and then she let out a terrifying screech—as Makail had expected. Her black eyes, nearly the size of Makail's head, pierced him. She had brown feathers surrounding her eyes, which faded into burgundy amassing her body and white-tipped wings. She was twice as thick as Makail with a wingspan exceeding twenty feet. To her screech, Makail cooed back. The gantor retracted her head and angled it, staring at Makail. The cooing persisted as he gently reached his hand toward one of her eggs. She watched making curious chirps and quarter-flapped her wings repeatedly. Makail softly grazed the egg with his fingertips and stretched his free arm toward the mother; she backed away, skittering around her nest to keep a distance. Eventually, Makail could feel her feathers. One feather equaled the width of Makail's hand, but he caressed them one by one. In doing this, the gantor could see Makail came as a friend meaning no harm, so he discontinued the cooing. The gantor never made another sound, and when she plopped on her eggs for the night, Makail used her as a soft feather mattress.

He woke to the prodding of the gantor's wing, causing him to quickly jumped off her back and pet her along the side, while saying "Thank you for giving me such a nice place to rest." The gantor opened her beak and let out a wary noise, like a distant train horn. Makail turned and crouched to hop on the mountain wall. After scaling all the way down to Queen Bidellia's castle, he jumped to the balcony, landing gently enough not to startle anyone. Tiptoeing across her balcony, he reached the window where he could peek in to see if she had woken. To his surprise, Fidelis stood at the doorway, speaking to Bidellia. Though Makail couldn't fully understand his every muffled word, he spoke of a guard's report that the queen had temporarily released a prisoner and the prisoner never returned. "You took an illmate from his cage!" his words shouted, begging for an explanation, but she replied calmly, and Makail could vaguely hear the words, "Just for a night." Which was followed by more stifled chatter from Fidelis, asking if he should have returned to his place. Makail had placed his ear to the wall, struggling to eavesdrop, and he heard her respond, "There was no further bid, for he had shown most everything he bears." With the ensuing comments, Fidelis inquired if they should send several guards to search for the man, and the queen smirked with an upward glance while shaking her head. Fidelis then asked what the queen would like to happen. She tilted her head to the side and toward the ceiling, crossing one arm across her waist with that wrist supporting her other arm's elbow, which led to her hand massaging her chin. After a moment, both arms collapsed to her side and she used her body language to say, It doesn't matter. The act forced Fidelis to react unkindly, growling, "You're much of no help on this matter, my queen," then closing the door with quiet authority.

Makail heard the door close and peaked through. Nobody else stood in her sprilen as the queen twirled his way, gently stepping toward her desk to continue with the work she'd begun the previous night, wearing her daily queen's attire. However, as she sat on her chair, Makail tapped the window, causing her too jump from her chair with wide, searching eyes. Scanning her room, she heard

Makail's whisper, "I'm over here, my queen, to speak with you."

"Makail," she murmured, puzzled.

"Correct," he said eagerly, yet quiet enough to stir no attention his way. Makail could see she had spotted him and begun walking his way. In a meek attempt to humor her, he added, "I hope you have no other man who might be tapping early morning panes."

The queen ignored his comment still seeming a bit confused. Though she knew he hadn't slept in his cage below her, which made her happy—for she didn't want him confined to such poor conditions any longer—she asked, "Whatever did you sleep amid?" hoping he at least slept last night.

"I slept up there inside a gantor nest. The mother ended up as warmly kind."

Bidellia began her chin toward Makail with her mouth slightly open, ready to speak then she jerked her head back as if stunned. Shaking her head with a smirk, she said, "You're strange indeed," as she left the door open for Makail to follow. She continued after Makail had crossed into her room and began shutting the door, "but I will also say, no god or goddess ever fancied such."

Makail took a moment to admire the room. Moving from his parents' hut to Quintix Valley, he'd never seen a more elaborate room. The space, the ceiling height, the bed size, wow! He hadn't noticed the room's beauty from outside. On the staircase to her bed, Bidellia had taken a seat on the third step with her feet on the first step. While gazing, Makail's sight wandered directly past her when he saw her pleasant eyes staring at him from a tilted head, allowing her blonde hair to dangle to her legs.

"Your beauty, well, no god could fancy such," he replicated for her own.

Gently blinking her eyes with the crack of a smile, she reiterated "I've never met a man who acts your way with all your strengths and nerve yet gentle touch."

"So happy me that you recall my touch." He paused briefly to gather his words. "If only I could figure out a way," gawking around the room before recentering Bidellia in his vision who anticipated his words, "to see that you may always cherish this."

Letting out a deep sigh, Bidellia kept her focus on Makail, who appeared embarrassed by his own remark. She felt compassionate toward him after last night with a tinge of remorse for leaving the way she had. Her attempt to comfort him came in the form, "You bleed the purest blood of Pithlyn blue, so I may see myself to cherish you."

He looked to the floor, hiding his face-wide smile.

Without glancing up he said, "I have no words expressing how I feel, but when you say such lovely words to me, I think I understand my parents' call." He looked up toward Bidellia, straightening his lips, "But first, I'd like to hear about your past."

Her eyes narrowed, thinking of how his parents had a great role in her more recent past. "About my past?" she questioned. To that, his brows raised with one head nod. For clarity, she offered, "what would you like to hear?"

"I know you've been alive for time by time, so tell me of the good and bad through time. I want to hear the stories of your life; it's plain: what makes you proud within your reign; what makes you fierce and more intemperate? What have you done, my queen, impressing most?" He stared at her, and to him, she seemed to be mulling through her past, trying to decipher exactly which stories to tell. As a reminder, he concluded, "I'd like to hear the good and bad of past, if only it may bring a closeness here—for me to understand the person here."

She smiled, rising to her feet. She walked toward the door Fidelis had recently closed, and Makail's heart began sinking a little. His first thought was, she's walking away again. His worry transformed dramatically when she latched the lock on the door so no other could disturb the two of them. Her calm smile fastened, as she walked across her room in front of Makail who watched with expecting stares.

She paced her room a few times before beginning, "I'm queen and Living Goddess for the live. With words, I grant men courage, never fear."

Queen Bidellia had only begun explaining portions of herself to Makail when he decided to inquisitively interject, as if to challenge her remark, "But fear could heave me to a hero's height."

Bidellia shot him a glare, for nobody interrupted the Living Goddess. "I'll talk," she demanded. Makail motioned that she has the floor, so she continued. "Men battle with their souls that thrive. In Favally, we won to share the grass; I've marched my troops across the Clatter Crest to battle gargentwans of Glaci Mass and win allegiance from the quasi-quest. To Zyder Mass, we crunched them ledge to ledge, yet still they're loyal to the north command where land, from us is pinched, declines from edge, as God of Peace had clinched and ripped the land. And now, we have the Threatle Gap to keep Dymetrice distant—they're our crudest creep."

Her pacing ceased as she'd disclosed to the extent of her wishes. She positioned herself in front of Makail by several feet. In awe, Makail had watched the entire time she spoke, taking in the stories she briefly shared. Her bravery and heroic leadership prevailed through her words. As a youth, he'd dreamed of doing special deeds with his immense array of skills. Queen Bidellia, without any great powers beyond her eternal flesh and blood coupled with her command and respect of all, had conquered many great feats. To lead her men confidently into battle, knowing the outcome would come in bloodshed or laudable agreements, she must be nothing less than extraordinary.

"Your tales could grip the soul of any man, and I, for one, have stood amazed by you." Makail peered to the floor, jostling his bare feet when he continued, "I never mentioned this to you before, but when I first set eyes on you from high atop the castle roof, I thought within, There's never been more beauty on a soul, and now I see, your beauty deepens more."

She glimmered toward him with an air of uncertainty. Uncertain of Makail's truth; uncertain if another man could feel this way for her; uncertain why he speaks to her like no man ever has; uncertain why he'd said he survived for her; uncertain if he'd always survive for her. She returned, "You're charming, like a child who praises me, but in a manly way as nature's gleam."

"I'm glad you left it not as me a child," he replied, smiling.

"You're not a child, that's very plain to see," letting out a breath of laughter, before finishing, "it's like the gods have sent you from a dream." She'd stepped closer to Makail as she spoke.

With only inches separating his chin from her nose, he admitted, "I love your Pithlyn passion, breath, and eyes, as you're more dreamlike than a childish dream."

She lifted her hand to his chest, really touching him for the first time. She could feel his strength, as if he could resist the greatest force. His heart beat where her fingers lightly grazed, and she noted the rapidity of its patter. "Your chest is of the mountains with a beat. Your eyes are of the leafless trees with snow." She paused her words to gently caress Makail's chin with her nose. "Your scent is of a manly smell, but sweet."

Finding his breath as her closeness made him tremble, he commented, "Your smell is of the healing pedals scent." He took a deep inhale, confessing, "My mouth may moisten any time your near, while yearning dearly for our lips to touch."

Bidellia cocked her head back to meet his eyes, and she sighed with, "Your sweetness deepens where my love may grow."

Makail countered, "My love had swelled for you while locked away, and now, to see and touch, my soul is free." He brought his hand up to her hair to brush it behind her ear. "I fell in love with you on first of sights, and I could love you till the end of time."

Queen Bidellia regained a hold of herself, realizing

she was melting away for a man she'd thrown to the bleak and had only really met the night before. She stepped back from Makail. As she did so, Makail felt the same pang in his chest as he had last night. He never wanted them to split apart like that. He felt as though he could be close to her every moment for the rest of his life. Yet, she'd turned her back to Makail, and he listened as she spoke, hoping to find answers in her words, "I can't subject myself to loving yet, for ugly endings come when moving fast, which turn a lovely love to soon regret." Turning her head over her shoulder to meet his eyes, she offered, "so tell of coming here, or recent past."

"Of coming here," he said most curiously, wondering if her attempts were to understand more of him before allowing herself to fall in love. He convinced himself of the notion, and willingly proceeded. "I came by naked foot. I met a kinder man of Pithlyn Mass when shortly crossing past the Pithlyn Gates. This man, named Gonko, warmly took me in and gave me rest, a meal, and then he healed."

As the word healed came from his mouth, her expression grazed perplexity, and he apprehended his omission of the Dymetrice Wall incident. Thus, Makail filled in the queen, "I had a wound, you see, along my side," caressing his right side. Bidellia watched with a different look on her face—a face of concern. Makail noticed her worried eyes, but continued on, assuming her concern stemmed from his battle. "A throttled scar reminding me I'd won a battle with the gargentwans on guard. Dymetrice Wall consisted of the two. At first, my main attempt was friendly-willed, but they were wicked souls inciting clash, so with my sword, I blocked the rapid hacks, except for one. Obtaining ground, I tossed them in the deep; a wave then took them out."

"Then with this fight, you did not end the men?" she responded.

"I had no reason as their cause of death. I simply had to make it past their shield."

"Do sing our praise, we're off to war again," she whispered.

"Whatever could you mean by war, my queen?" blatantly confused.

"It's better if you leave at once, Makail."

"I do not understand the trouble here; I merely overcame a barricade to carry on my course to Pithlyn Mass."

"The trouble here is they are coming," she expressed with the subtlety the queen has always possessed when her land reached imminent danger. She ordered, "Leave!"

Prepare

From her mission to Glaci, a couple hundred years ago, which she had just mentioned to Makail, Queen Bidellia understood the mentality of the gargentwans. She had marched her troops beyond the Clatter Crest after hearing of their recent commitment to assist Dymetrice in all matters concerning protection, security, and confrontation. A vast army followed her, intending to prove her seriousness, as the queen knew she would either convince the gargentwan leader—Hilbrus at the time—to revoke his loyalties to Dymetrice or she and her men would spread gargentwan blood until Hilbrus surrendered and reconsidered his priorities.

Hilbrus had agreed to the allegiance with Dymetrice because they had promised the gargentwans an ample supply of wood for fires at all times. Queen Bidellia countered with, "We'll serve your men with wood and loyal aid to be a team with you through good and bad." Hilbrus had recognized a friendly offer with a thinking face. "And that Dymetrice promise soon will fade and leave you cold without the friend you had."

Hilbrus retorted, "They will not fulfill our promise. How could we have been duped? They wanted us for our size. Dymetrice does not care about us." He had continued to think aloud, rumbling through a multitude of reasons supporting Queen Bidellia's claims, before finishing, "We will always avenge a traitor." Such a line echoes through the Glaci mountains for all generations. Nobody crosses gargentwans without repercussions; they have always fought back for prideful statements, and in this past case, gargentwans stormed through Dymetrice, igniting forests, tormenting villages, and gashing through King Avel's castle, threatening his life—all for a misunderstanding.

Despite his yearning to stay with Bidellia, Makail fulfilled her demands, solemnly leaving her room. Once he'd vanished from her castle's proximity, she quickstepped through her door and burst into Fidelis's room. "Fidelis," she addressed, "come with Dux."

Fidelis fled on his queen's order, rushing down the corridor and up the first flight of stairs. Dux, as leader-under-queen of all her armies, lived behind the first door on the hall consisting of single guards who turn soldier when battle impends. Fidelis knocked with a flurry, and Dux slowly reached the door to crack it open. Dux had yet to put on a shirt for the day, so he stood in a way Fidelis could only see his face. With bulging eyes, Fidelis exclaimed, "Come, we must meet with the queen immediately."

"What's with your fright?" Dux asked.

Fidelis paused. "I don't know." "But the queen acted with urgency."

"On Omnerce, you are to the queen as a shummy is to momma grilk." Dux said lightly while turning to retrieve a shirt. Starting to pull the shirt over his head, he justified his comment, "The queen gets proud, you jubilate; the queen gets disturbed, you become nervous; the queen acts with urgency, you're flustered; the queen remains calm, you're transparent."

"Enough already, close it." he replied calmly, "You know it's my job to act for her and as her."

Sarcastically, Dux said, "That does mean you must reflect her feelings at all times. For your sake, I hope she never hikes to love for a man." He swung his door open to follow Fidelis to Queen Bidellia's room. Through the corridor, Dux continued mumbling for Fidelis to hear, "This had better be important. I was planning on taking some time to walk to the Deep and swim with the fish or flounder near them. Tomorrow I thought I'd hike up the old mountain path to see where I would have swum yesterday, which is actually this day." Then he quickly verbalized a change in thoughts, "What could she possibly find so urgent for you to be in such a tizzy?"

They had reached the door to Queen Bidellia's room, and with his hand on the handle, Fidelis turned back to Dux, "The queen has reasons."

In her room, she paced along the floor opposite the door where Fidelis and Dux entered. Each took their normal chair at the meeting table while Queen Bidellia acted unaware they had arrived. Her mind toiled over the gargentwans avenging Makail's escape of Dymetrice. Would they feel the need to battle due to the incident? If so, because the act occurred on Dymetrice soil, would the gargentwans invite the Dymetrice army to fight with them? She also considered the size of the gargentwans and their ability to shake off nearly any opposition. At once, Queen Bidellia dashed her head toward the two men, continuing her thoughts, she stated, "We must prevail."

Taken aback, Dux questioned, "How can we prevail without a competition?" obviously unaware of any forthcoming.

Of course, Fidelis had no details on the queen's thoughts by this point, but he had a steadfast conviction that all the queen's concerns revolved around the escaped prisoner in one way or another. "Please, my queen, elaborate on our necessary prevailance."

"This time we have is but a quick reprieve before the storms of masses raid the east," she said, walking to the table to sit with the other two.

Dux quickly jigged his thoughts, "You mean Dymetrice is coming!" With hardly a pause for any response, he included, "Let's head east. Now, that sounds more invigorating than swimming or hiking," slapping Fidelis on the chest. "I've been craving a chance to rip apart each of them since my first day here."

"Be calm," the queen declared before explaining, "the gargentwans have bent on us because Makail defeated two."

"Makail…?" Dux wondered, "Who's Makail?" looking wide-eyed from Fidelis to the queen.

Fidelis let him know, "Makail is a man from Dymetrice whom the queen ordered to the dungeon for impeding our progress to Favally some time ago. The queen took the captive for a walk last night, and he has not returned. I knew the unworthy scum was up to no good!"

Dux squinted his eyes at Fidelis, "Unworthy? How is one man who defeats two gargentwans at once unworthy? It takes an army to befall a single gargentwan."

"He's not…" Fidelis became fuddled, previously

unaware of Makail's power. Dux's statement carried truth, and Fidelis knew such a feat ranked as unfathomable. However, Fidelis could not allow himself to praise the man, so he countered, "He's a Dymetrice man! He has no duty here."

The queen had listened to the two bicker then she continued, "At least, they'll start to fight from their defeat, and thus, they'll force their forces from Dymetrice Wall. We must remain to hope Dymetrice stays, or else too many Pithlyn men will fall."

"As if the gargentwans alone would not slaughter so many of our fleet," Dux added.

Fidelis shared his thoughts with the quaint table, "Of course Dymetrice will join the gargentwans in this battle! Makail, that lowly prisoner, planned it all! He is for Dymetrice, and once this fray begins, he'll be ready to turn on all of us. We must find the man; we must press him back to his quarters. He's the one who started this all, and if we don't find him first, he'll attempt to finish this."

She directed her voice to Fidelis, "Such claims describe a daunting, haunting haze." The queen felt obliged to confess for the lowly prisoner, "Makail pumps Pithlyn blood."

"What makes you believe in this, my queen?" Fidelis returned.

Chapter 15

"What's all the fuss for some lowly who escaped?" Dux intervened. "Send me out to find him. I'll bring him back in time for lunch."

She mainly ignored Dux remark and answered Fidelis, though not revealing everything she'd come to understand about Makail. She kept her words to, "The flowers tell."

"If the flower sticks…" Dux deemed under his breath.

"The Goddess of Healing honors this Dymetrice man?" After the queen nodded her head, Fidelis continued, "Perhaps his ancestors, or even parents, come from Pithlyn, but he was raised Dymetrice. His loyalties are to Dymetrice! He said it himself, 'I'm Makail of Dymetrice." remember my queen? He is here to befriend us then defeat us."

His comments sent the queen to a guardrail of frightening thoughts. Makail had acted kindly and sweetly toward her, which allowed for Fidelis's words to make sense. Makail's evil intentions infuriated the queen, but on the surface, she appeared calm, not listening to the two men discuss their ideas. Dux primarily focused on his desire to obliterate any loyal Dymetrice muck willing to fight against him, acting eager to draw his sword. Fidelis carried on with his lack of trust for Makail and any other Dymetrice born who crosses the Pithlyn threshold.

Prepare

Ending her silence, Queen Bidellia declared, "Prepare the troops and bang the battle bell. At once, this meeting here is now adjourned. I'll find Makail." She let out a sigh, as if a difficult task loomed. Even though she knew he'd come back to her, she added, "with help from gods above."

Fidelis left with Dux, and once the door to her room had closed, her trembling hands clinched, lips tightened, chin quivered. She wanted to flip her room upside down in disturbed anger; she wanted to cry and scream to the gods for playing so foul; she wanted to not believe Fidelis's accusations on Makail's intentions. Spending one short night with him revealed enough for her to understand his excessive idiosyncrasies. Makail did not tremor away from the queen like everybody else. He stood with confidence and a whole heart for her. Queen Bidellia had begun to fall in love with the Pithlyn-blooded Makail of Dymetrice. But she had to put her mass first. Besides, what had Makail provided to prove his love for her? Neither great buoyancy nor a melodic song could prove the depths of love Queen Bidellia had sought for centuries. Only one way existed for Makail to prove love for Bidellia.

After he had followed Queen Bidellia's demands, leaving her room, Makail had scaled to the summit of a nearby mountain to rest in complete solitude. The way a boy dwells over his current crush, atop the mountain Makail had kept an even picture of Bidellia in his mind while Fidelis and Dux had discussed with the queen of an ensuing battle. Makail also considered his parents' words, his mission to find Queen Bidellia, as she would keep him safe. To this point, Makail still had no idea what his parents had meant by Queen Bidellia keeping him safe. He knew he'd found the queen, but what to do next remained an uncharted path. His parents had dialed a lengthy path for him, but they could not write his entire story, for they could not foresee his exact actions; they could not gauge his future emotions; they could not force him to act as they wish; they could only hope he would and prepare him to make the right decisions. Following his parents' lead had brought him to this point, where he would need to make the decisions on his own.

Attempting to see his next move, he could only think of Bidellia—her gentle smile, her soft eyes after he'd sung to her, her wavy hair, her trim physique, her enthralling appearance. On the summit Makail realized Bidellia possessed more than any woman he'd ever meet. Her beauty exceeded everything. And he could not bear another day without seeing her.

Gargentwans

During Makail's stay in the confinary of Pithlyn's castle—so while Queen Bidellia errantly traveled through Favally—the gargentwans Makail had fought off had swum to the Dymetrice coast south of the wall where the shore met waves without any cliff. This route presented a shorter distance than swimming back to their point of liftoff, and no cliff to climb made it even more reasonable. The two hadn't landed side by side of course, and after Makail's wave sent them deeper into the deep, they further separated. Each of them, however, thought along the same lines.

Tyban had reached the shore first, lowering to his hands and knees with his brawny chest bulging then shrinking. Junder followed shortly, yet he wound up a mile south of Tyban. Each trekked back to the wall alone, but when Junder arrived to their original position,

Tyban had awaited. The two exchanged a few quick sentences, outlining future fate. Even though the ride ahead of them had proven arduous, they knew no choice existed in the matter. Gargentwan code made an enemy of one who disregards their word and disparages their abilities.

They'd packed all the food they had left into a large sand-colored bag with leather drawstrings and hoisted the sack into the back of their boat, although they didn't actually need the food. Because of their mammoth size, they could store enough nutrients to last an extended period of time, similar to a bear preparing for hibernation. Their boat had rested at the north edge of Dymetrice Wall. From there, the two raised their boat, carrying it further north until they could walk directly from land to water. Considering the construction of this boat, Tyban and Junder needed to walk it into the water carefully on its side. Tyban held the boat end while Junder took the bottom of the waterwheel structure.

The gargentwans believed a wheel churning water underneath a boat would allow for a more effective and efficient ride. Only the gargentwans possessed enough manly power to operate these oversized unicycle canoes. The wheel had a diameter of twenty-three feet, meaning roughly a seventy-two-foot circumference, which held twenty-four evenly-spaced paddles angled perfectly to cut through the water for enhanced speeds. The only thing connecting the wheel to the boat were four sturdy iron beams linked from the outer center point of the wheel's axel, which rotated on a circle equivalent to the circumference of the pedal's boundaries. In the canoe's middle, these pedals were covered by a wooden box with only a couple spaces on two sides for the feet of the two sweaters. Underneath the box, the base of the canoe slanted toward the water, preventing any excessive leakage.

As the two had lugged their vessel into neck-level water, Junder released the wheel from hand. He swam forward and toward the boat's side, joining Tyban. Junder then had a hold of the front tip while Tyban carried the rear, as they swam to deep enough waters for the wheel to straighten without touching the deep's bottom. This method allowed for them to properly angle the wheel slowly more toward the bottom of the deep. Once the boat appeared to float normally, Junder dog-paddled to the opposite side, and the two climbed in simultaneously to prevent tipping, although the wheel made it more difficult to actually tip.

Once the two had begun spinning the pedals and handles, Tyban had, "We are moving the wrong way."

Junder had responded, "We should switch directions." Before the water became shallow enough for the wheel to

Chapter 16

hit bottom, they had reversed directions to head toward Glaci. This boat required heavily pressing feet at first, but once paddles began to routinely slice through the water, the boat glided on silk with speeds exceeding sixty miles per hour, making for one breezy ride. Traveling through the Gelid Deep from their Dymetrice coast to the northern part of Glaci Mass would last eight grinding days.

When they had arrived to Glaci, they immediately sought Hilbran, heading to the leader's lair. The mouth of Hilbran's lair raised twenty-five feet high, carrying a width of ten feet. Snow and ice encased the opening. Inside the trail led straight before turning right for several gargentwan strides when it turned left. A few strides after the second turn, the lair broadened to suit a king. Despite the tunnel's shadowed walls, torches brightened Hilbran's arena, revealing a spacious ring decorated with jewels and paintings of past leaders and heroes.

Hilbran saw his two men walk into his light and asked, "What brings you two from your guard on Dymetrice Wall?"

Tyban spoke, "We request permission to request Dymetrice's allegiance to battle Pithlyn."

Stunned, Hilbran narrowed his eyes, "Our loyalties are with Queen Bidellia. Our loyalties are with Pithlyn

Mass. Why would we want to team with Dymetrice? Why would we want to attack Pithlyn?"

Tyban explained, "A man from Dymetrice beat us. He made it to Pithlyn."

"One man cannot defeat the both of you at once."

"He threw us in the deep!" Junder intervened, receiving impatient stares from each.

Tyban went on, "He must be more than a man. We attacked him at once. He blocked away everything we had."

"Why attack Pithlyn? A Dymetrice man defeated you."

"He wanted to go to Pithlyn. He told us that. We think it is his homeland," Tyban answered.

"It must be his homeland," Junder added.

"One man got past you. You want to start a war?"

Tyban attempted to reassure his leader, "It was the way he did it. He rebelled against us. He disregarded our orders. The orders are your orders."

Hilbran considered Tyban. Tyban had always demonstrated excellent decision making. He fought with his heart, following gargentwan code, fighting for his people. Hilbran opened, "He crossed us. He crossed our demands. He crossed what we stand for. Now we must stand for vengeance."

"I will let the rest of us know that we will fight with

Dymetrice," Tyban responded.

"I will too," Junder notched just before Hilbran could command.

"No you won't. Our loyalties are with Queen Bidellia and Pithlyn. I will never battle her army. Many of us feel the same way. You will ask your fellows if they will walk in war beside you."

"We will," Tyban submitted.

"You will bring your fighting men back with you. I will assign our ships for you. You will meet with King Avar. You will let him know the circumstance."

Tyban and Junder nodded, and Hilbran flipped his hand to them, signing them out. Over the next couple days, the two had spoken to all near six hundred male gargentwans. Most of them desired to keep their loyalties with Queen Bidellia; however, more than one hundred and fifty of them united for battle. As instructed, Tyban met with Hilbran once he'd assembled a crew. Hilbran assigned the two largest ships for their retreat, and Tyban would serve as the honorary leader. After final blessings from Hilbran, the gargentwans had set sail for a six-day journey to the northern coast of Dymetrice, which had gone without a hitch.

After the voyage, the herd of gargentwans cluttered the coast as Tyban held attention of all. He called out to them, "We have one mission here. Seven of us will stay here to guard the ships. The rest will walk together. I will meet with King Avar alone. I will ask him to join us in battle. He will accept my offer." "We will pass many villages. People will fear us. We will tell them we seek mutuality. We will tell them we are friends." Tyban turned his back to the rest and began walking south. This march had lasted six more days, and on the day Tyban would meet with King Avar, he commanded his crew to hold back in a nearby forest, just beyond the slim mountains surrounding Dymetrice's castle. These slim mountains did not hold the shape of ordinary mountains; rather, they sprung to the sky, like medieval jousting sticks, breathing a dusty red. They were not packed tightly or rising in any particular order. These spikes simply rose at random with a large dusty red expanse between them.

Tyban walked to the castle door with his battle boots collected the reddish color of that terrain. Four guards attempted insubstantial defense of the castle door, but when Tyban demanded to see King Avar, raising his thunderous voice, they all squirmed into the castle, informing King Avar of his visitor, and leaving the door unattended. Tyban ducked his head and entered. He waited just inside the front door, looking around the dim room with red walls, as if it were constructed of the same material as the mountains. A dozen flame-lit lanterns hung from the walls, and wooden chairs took to the floor as spontaneously as the castle's surrounding mountains.

From around a corner on the opposite side of this large opening room, King Avar appeared, "What is it you want from me?"

"My name is Tyban," he rumbled. "I come to seek your hand in battle."

"Who is at war?" he asked, clearly fuddled.

"There is no war for now. We must avenge disrespect. A Pithlyn man made a mockery of us. We must send a message through the cries of Pithlyn kind. I have one-fifty of my men ready for battle."

King Avar kept a kingly appearance, notwithstanding his deepest delight of entering a battle with Pithlyn foe. He further questioned, "You want to go to war with an entire mass because of banter?"

"One man represents the whole. He threw us in the Carné Sea. His entire mass shall pay for such insolence."

King Avar's eyes strained with a piqued mouth. He wondered, who in this sphere could possibly launch a gargentwan to water? "Take a seat," hesitating, realizing Tyban would not fit in any of the chairs lined along the walls, "anywhere you'd like within this room. I will speak with my committee at once, and we will promptly make you aware of our decision." Something had become amiss. Thus, King Avar had made up his mind before meeting with his committee, which meant his meeting sparked debate of the proper plan for attack.

Waiting in the foyer, Tyban clinched his fists, punching them together. Three men passed him, nodding their heads in simple, hurried acknowledgement before leaving the castle. His anxiety grew, for he couldn't overcome his craving to punish those who crossed him and his kind. As his disdain simmered, King Avar entered his sight line to declare, "We will stand with you, but we will fight by my orders. Since you've come to speak with me, I can safely assume Hilbran stayed in Glaci; therefore, I'm the leader of our legion." Tyban continued to listen, fuming with adrenaline. "Your ships must be on the north shore. Ours are south. Our fleet is vaster than any other mass on this sphere. We have large ships for warring, mid-size ships for exploring east, and a variety of smaller ships for intentioned voyages. You will send two of your men down to me to travel on one of our smaller ships to Zyder. Trust me, our smaller ships will comfortable fit a couple of gargentwans. Your two men will alert Zyder of our battle. Floating in on one of my ships will set them at ease; they will listen and obey your men as the orders come from me. Zyder forces will be directed to head north. Zyder's men will travel beyond the Simmery Gorge, traipse right through the golden wall because all those guards will be fighting us, and then Zyder will wind along the southern Pithlyn mountains where they will eventually see us battling. You see, we will have every Pithlyn man's attention, but then from the south we catch them off guard with another wave of legion! They will not stand a chance. And if we can conquer them enough, I will rule over Pithlyn, for I will not cease the fight until that Living Goddess bows to me and calls me her king.

"As for your troops, head back to your ships, bring them all the way around our coast and through the Straits of Silony. We will meet by water there. Our entry point to Pithlyn will be on the south side of Pithlyn Point. Your fleet will advance from ours. Your men will touch first ground and march! If Pithlyn is not ready for us, we make them bleed. Your men will lead us through as the first line of warriors to be defeated by nobody. Any questions?"

Tyban had heard everything. Knowing the assigned duty of his men, his lack of clarity solely rested on something else: "Your ships are south. Many of your villages are west. How will you band enough men to fight Pithlyn?"

"Well, this battle seems to present a surprise for the other side. I don't think we will need much more than a few well-trained men and your flock to defeat them. With that said, however, I'm planning on a massacre, so I sent a few other men west. These men have each trained their own gantor, and they can ride them easier than most can ride a raxar. They will gather our fighters and send them south. Our ships will sail close to shore to scoop these waiting fighters from the coast. By the time we meet up with you at the base of Dymetrice Point, we'll have enough troops to diminish not just Pithlyn, but Favally and Indiffron too. Since this is a surprise attack, though, we shouldn't have to worry about any joined forces."

"Your words come true. My men will be ready. We will be waiting at Threatle Gap," Tyban finished. When Tyban turned his back to King Avar, a smile raised his cheeks.

With a quickened step, Tyban walked the near three miles back to the desolate woodland where his fellow men had remained. An overpouring of excitement and anxiety ran through him, and he could not hide his jubilance after King Avar's agreement. Of course the gargentwans would comply with leading the way and front-lining the battle. This tribe reveled in leading, especially when it was for their own cause. The gargentwans were a proud group, so to lead battle only fueled their existing adrenaline.

When he reached his lingering army, he informed all of his meeting with King Avar and the instructions to fulfill. Tyban's men reflected his own emotions, and before heading back for their ships, Tyban raised his left arm with an open palm. The others mirrored his lead, raising the right hands with an open palm. Before his clan, He announced, "You will follow me. We will lead the way in this battle. We will fight. We will emerge in victory!"

Wave

Sitting on his summit seat, the battle bell disrupted Makail's thoughts. He bounced to his feet, listening intently to the faint sounds of repeated dongs ricocheting through the mountains. Everything inside him sunk a little, wondering what could be the cause of a bell. He'd never heard this sound before, so he feared the worst, feeling it couldn't mean anything positive. With his desire to show concern for Bidellia and intent to present himself for help, he chested the mountain wall to quickly scale downward to the queen's balcony.

Reaching the necessary point on the mountain, Makail leaped to the balcony and crept to the opening into Bidellia's room. He poked his head around its corner to see her sitting at the table, softly sobbing dryly. In a whisper, he asked, "My queen, if all is clear, what's with that bell?"

Chapter 17

She turned a narrow glare to him and hastily rose from her chair, storming through her room and out the door. She'd heard Fidelis return to his room a few moments prior after he'd ordered a guard to bang the bell. Thus, she knocked on his door. When he acknowledged his own presence, she cracked open his door and headed back to her room. Such an action was common for Queen Bidellia when she needed Fidelis to meet with her in her room, so Fidelis followed suit, following in her tracks.

When Bidellia reentered her room, Makail stood at the base of her bed. "Has something troubled you since last we met?"

The queen tilted her chin closer to her chest, unable to sight the man her soul desired. As she did so, Fidelis appeared in the doorway with a look of alarmed disdain. Fidelis, said "The Dymetrice scum has been found again. Excellent work, my queen. I don't understand how you found him so quickly."

Bidellia raised her head, peering to the ceiling with her deepest inhale followed by a gradual exhale. She said nothing, anxious for Fidelis to detain Makail.

Fidelis continued with his voice aimed to Makail, "Back to the confinary for you. Until this battle you've caused is over, you will never see release."

"What battle have I caused without intent?"

Her highest eyes lifted at Makail's words, as she wondered of truth within his words. Had her trusted nobleman been misled within his own head? But she had to believe Fidelis, as his loyalties and respect over the years had never strayed. Fidelis had walked to Makail's back and tightened his hands around Makail's side-hanging wrists from behind. He began coercing Makail out of the room, while stating, "You know what you've done. Don't act dumber than a raxar's secretion."

"Oh, what's the meaning here?" Makail demanded. Turning his attention to Bidellia as they approached her position, he softened, whispering "My queen, my love, it's you I'd love with soul for all of time, if you could have my hand for all of time."

For the first time since Fidelis had entered, Queen Bidellia looked at Makail. She reached to his arm, grabbing it, causing Fidelis to halt and release the right wrist. She stared deep into his eyes, forcing herself to believe her own words when she said, "Unproven love can never be returned."

Still gripping her eyes with his, he begged, "My queen, how might I prove my love for you."

Holding her stare as if she expected the question, she revealed, "The love for Pithlyn Mass would prove your love."

Clearly annoyed by the whispers, Fidelis torqued his

ratched hand, initiating Makail's onward movement past the queen when he regripped the right wrist. Makail moved his lips, trying to say something, but he merely audibled stuttered grunts. In an attempt to show his displeasure with going back to the confinary, he struggled with Fidelis's grip until they'd left Bidellia's room. Yet, Makail continued to annoy Fidelis through the corridor and down the steps, desperately attempting his honest claims.

After returning Makail to his cage, Fidelis charged back to Bidellia's room to interrogate. She sat at her desk, staring blankly at its surface, as he asked, "What was the meaning of your nonsense whispers to that villain?"

The queen never turned her back from Fidelis, who stood with one foot on the first step of the staircase to Bidellia's bed. "He's kind to me, yet bold and daring too."

At her words, he realized she didn't find Makail; rather, he came back to her. And with her melancholy words, he felt a twinge that she might believe Makail came as the right man for her. "You cannot reduce to loving this man!" he demanded. "He is of the other side; he caused the battle for which we must now prepare."

Queen Bidellia shrugged her shoulders then peered over them. "You know I'd never love the traitor kind."

She stood from her chair and began walking prominently to her door. Maintaining her stride, she walked into the corridor refocusing her energies on the assumed forthcoming battle, yelling back to Fidelis, "Now there's a massive fleet we must subdue, and even worse if all our foes combined."

Fidelis scurried to keep pace with the queen, "What do you mean all our foes combined?"

"Dymetrice, Glaci, even Zyder might join force and form a legion vast as all."

Stepping quickly, Fidelis worked like a faselot hunter to remain a stride behind the queen, as she sashayed through the main entry room and out the main doors. The two sped down the rock steps, ending in the grassy bottom where they'd wait for the three nearby authoritators from Pithly, Nearo, and Vafarm. These authoritators' duty in response to the battle bell, which resonates well enough for keen ears in those three villages, involved meeting the queen in the foreground of her castle to discuss approach, strategy, and opposition. Such a gathering typically ended quickly: the queen's orders followed by the authoritators acquiescence.

Soren, of Pithly, arrived by raxar first. As tradition, he waited for Lakse of Nearo and Gerim of Vafarm before crossing the stream to meet at eye with the queen. After a few moments, Lakse's raxar scooted into position next to Soren's. The two exchanged acknowledgement then faced straight ahead. Gerim straggled in much later than the other two, sending an apology for his own delay. Soren and Lakse nodded heads and the three stepped their raxars over the river to receive an order from the Living Goddess.

Queen Bidellia wasted no moments in demanding, "We'll send our wave due east where we will fight the largest beast, so take your best and stall no more, for war is soon."

"Dymetrice invades," Fidelis explained. "The queen believes Dymetrice will not come alone, as the gargentwans feel they've been crossed by a man now residing in our dungeon. The gargentwans, knowing their mentality, will have asked Dymetrice to join forces. With Zyder's loyalties and awe to Dymetrice, we have no reason to believe Zyder won't join them as well. We could be facing our largest battle yet!"

Soren questioned, "Do we have enough men to challenge such an immense army?"

"My league has heft," Queen Bidellia began, "to battle on till all the opps have left. We'll fight for Pithlyn's breath, which gives to most the courage bold enough to fight enraged. So let us battle best at Carné Coast and slay the beast without our deaths so staged!"

"Our queen!" Soren shouted, slipping his sword from

its carrier on his raxar's side and raising it toward the gods.

"Commence the wave!" Lakse announced, matching Soren's sword.

"To fight as one!" Gerim finished, brining a third sword to the air.

The raxars peeled away, charging through the aisle between flowers, hustling to their respected towns. The wave begins with a ripple as Soren, Gerim, and Lakse individually alert those of their home towns. The ripple builds a current as the three continue their separate paths. As the current progresses with increasing numbers, momentum builds, rising to the crest of their wave. The crest is meant to flow from Fiwel, where all groups combine to form one massive army, to Endefder. In Endefder, the entire Pithlyn army stands ready to crash with enemy forces.

The primary courses Soren, Gerim, and Lakse take is called a splitoff group. Soren begins south, collecting men from villages south and east of the queen's castle. After six days, his building crew rounds the Lake of Pithlyn before slanting northeast toward Fiwel. From Vafarm, Gerim moves the men of his village northeast, until reaching the central bridge over the Pithlyn River where they turn southward for a couple days before straightening their path toward Fiwel. After Lakse gathers his men from Mofdar, he takes them north, and by the sixth day, they will have reached Pithlyn's northern coast where they turn east and cross the northernmost bride of the Pithlyn River. Hanging near that northern coast, Lakse's group bears east, hedging south before drawing parallel with Clatter Crest to head toward Fiwel. All three splitoff groups shed with splinter groups. As the splitoff steadies toward a village along their course, splinter groups fetch from villages off the main course, reuniting farther into the splitoff's course. This allowed for no village to be passed, and by the end, every combatant in Pithlyn would stand guard with Endefder. It has been a war order for centuries.

Dux had given notice to his fellow members on the royal committee. Each member ran a deep background of grueling training as a fighter; any time a battle bubbled, the royal committee transformed from an intelligent decision-making team to a fearless army. After acquainting his committee members with this information, he informed the guards. During battles, a dozen guards stayed home while the other couple dozen always marched ready to attack any force against them.

As Soren and the other two rode off, Fidelis turned toward the stable to the south where a hundred raxars snorted and nayed while digesting breakfast. Queen Bidellia split from Fidelis and headed up the stairs to find peace within her room. Since the expeditions taken by Soren, Lakse, and Gerim would take much longer than that of the royal party, Queen Bidellia's crew, which stayed a straight course across Pithlyn, would wait five full days, allowing the others a head start to meet timely at Fiwel before marching as one to Endefder.

Fidelis met with the raxar's devoted caretakers inside the stable. Twenty men lived in huts surrounding the stable for easy access to their beloved raxars. Behind the stable, a great expanse provided room to train, run free, and play. During the gathering with Fidelis, he explained the battle at hand and the necessary imminent use of nearly every raxar in the stable. The caretakers understood the meaning of his words and the length of quick preparation for these enduring animals—a lot of rest, more food, and most of all a very large quantity of water.

During days prior to a known battle, nobody disturbed the queen, giving her serene study of strategy. On the first day, however, she could not think of a battle, only Makail. For most of the day, she paced along her balcony, feeling the sun's heat and glancing toward the illmates working around her castle. She noticed Makail chopping grass at the base of the steps, who'd been ordered to carry out this duty while others worked higher up the mountain, which meant every illmate would look down upon him. But Bidellia didn't think like that. She saw a sorrow man; a man capable of good things; a man with abilities far greater than her entire fleet combined; a man she could hold as her own equal. Makail hacked through the grass replaying the prior night. Had it really just been on the other side of the sun when he toyed with Bidellia where he currently mowed? Could it have really been just one blink of a night's rest since he sang her his song? Everything had turned since then. To him, it seemed as though he'd finally positioned everything to set up in his favor, then he's thrown back in the hollow cage to carry on as a hollow body. His mind tunnel-visioned his sight, never looking up, feeling ashamed of the location of his upbringing.

Though Bidellia had rested quietly that night, blocking out the graceful hum from beneath her, she awoke at sunrise in fear. Not fear for self but fear for those who would wage their own lives for the defense of Pithlyn. If the other army closed with great vastness as anticipated, would her legion stand a chance? How long could how many men stand against the raiding gargentwans? She vexed all day on questions regarding the strength of her army compared to the force against it. As her thoughts closed for the night, she stood on her balcony and asked the gods, "How might we win and what is Pithlyn's toll?"

After asking, she bowed her head and solemnly staggered to her room, up her steps, and into bed. She dreamed of battle that night. Gargentwans and Dymetrice troops overpowering her own; Pithlyn souls rising to the gods by the dozens. As she woke by morning, sweat splattered her forehead, dampening her hair. She jumped from her bed, rather than easing down the stairs, and rushed to her desk where she took out notes from another battle at Carpé Coast with the same foe minus gargentwans. One hundred and twelve years ago, Dymetrice fought with Zyder for reign over Pithlyn, which would have given then King Avol of Dymetrice absolute power over the entire sphere, and he would have been seen as the living god. Queen Bidellia had surrendered to save Pithlyn flesh, but on her captive ride to King Avol's castle, she laid out one requirement for him to purely take rule. He would have to defeat her in a dual, either by death or surrender, for the gods would never see him as the superior being unless he could defeat her. He conceded to her request, and after the dual, the next in line, King Avak took over in Dymetrice and sent Bidellia back to her mass as a victor.

The notes she studied during this second day of waiting were written the first day she arrived back to her castle after defeating King Avol. These notes had faded over time, but she could make it out for the most part, filling in the blanks with her extended memory. Dymetrice had flooded through Carpé Coast for the battle, leaving Endefder all but conquered. One man escaped from the attacked village, riding a raxar all the way to Queen Bidellia, only stopping to warn various villages on route. Yet, fourteen days of Dymetrice battling through Pithlyn communities had passed before a Pithlyn army clashed with them. And by the time Pithlyn clanked swords, Zyder's men had overwhelmed Queen Bidellia's grass. She read through her notes to remind herself of their methods in attack. Unless a revelation of weaponary had been created, Zyder would come with their throwing pierce—small metal balls with six six-inch spikes for penetration. Dymetrice would bring their spears—usually eight feet in height with a durable metal tip, used to throw into the enemy or stab them from a greater distance than the sword's reach. The gargentwans, she knew not from her notes, would carry their ringed spheres—like the two had at Dymetrice Wall. Each had those trademark weapons, along with the typical weapons of swords, knives, dense wooden sticks, and brass shields for protection.

By day's end, she knew what to expect from this attack. A hope of hers rested against the shortfall of not organizing her men quickly enough to arrive in Endefder before gargentwans and Dymetrice bashed through the village. Also, she spoke to the gods of Pithlyn warfare and durability of equipment, pleading, "Do let our steel exceed the steel of foes." Again, her dreams mared of Pithlyn deaths and euphoric gargentwans shaking hands with King Avar.

The following morning, she woke up shook up from her dream. Gathering her thoughts, she calmly dressed herself in her common queen's attire and floated to the training room inside the castle, which laid on the opposite side of the throne room from the queen's corridor and through doors on the wall behind the queen's chair. In this room, she quietly observed as men prepared earnestly for the ensuing battle, exercising in roborant ways, fine-tuning every tactic, and evaluating weapons for any quick repairs. Some guards and members sharpened blades in the blacksmith's room. Nothing could lack anything in the days leading up to battle, and Queen Bidellia's men knew this very well.

Witnessing her men's preparation furnished her thoughts with comfort, knowing their ambitions and common love for Pithlyn. Her men would exceed great lengths for their motherland. She felt their love so well, and yet they'd endanger everything for which they worked because of the imminent danger facing Pithlyn. So on this night, she looked above and exclaimed, "Great gods must guard my every Pithlyn soul." As her thoughts turned to dreams, Omnerce swiped his hand once across a black backdrop while gargentwans marched toward her men. Nearing the clash, flashes of a single man zipped through enemy warpaths, spoiling their attack.

She awoke in wonder. That flash of a man could have only been one man. She rushed herself to dressed and flurried out her castle, down the steps, and to the stable. Fidelis always focused a great deal of his attention on overseeing the raxar's preparation for their grueling days of travel. Queen Bidellia charged to the stables, assuming he'd already be watching over the caretakers. She stepped through the dirt path down the center of the stable, searching left and right at each cross path. Fidelis spoke with a caretaker from a stable door when the queen spotted him. She approached him silently, catching the corner of his eye. Slightly ducking his head, he said, "My queen." "You look a bit bewildered this morning. Is something troubling you?"

"Makail," she said softly.

"What? Has he escaped again?"

She tightened her fist, thumping her thigh, "We cannot win unless he goes."

"And have some Dymetrice born rat defusing the battle for us, surrendering hard-trained men to the enemy. It's a ludicrous risk, and I advise against it with everything I have. We cannot trust that man, and he hasn't proven himself for anything, most likely because all he can prove is his desire for Dymetrice to dominate the world."

"My feelings feel like you are very wrong, but you've been fair, and I will trust in you."

"Thank you, my queen. You know my intentions are only for the good of Pithlyn Mass," he finished.

She nodded her head and began walking back to the center aisle of the stable. As she stood in the cross path, she turned to Fidelis, reminding him, "With morrow's morning, we shall take our strong to battle till triumphant through and through."

Fidelis smiled, "Yes my queen, Pithlyn will triumph."

After her day scrutinizing past battles to help her understand the anticipated, she walked to her balcony. The sky shaded the darkest blue one could ever imagine with a large, brightly glowing circle, outlined by its own penumbra. The stars shone in full bloom through the quiet air. She spoke, "The stars shine brightly. They're my father's eyes, which say, we'll never meet with our demise." Pivoting back to her room, she fell asleep by the soft hums from below. That night, she dreamed of winning…with the aid of gods.

Current

Onward, they marched, multiplying by the day. Splitoff groups rallied troops from villages to which the authoritators' crews never came close. The splitoffs reunited with authoritators a few days later with more men on each side. The armies met then split, met then split, met then split, each time gathering greater numbers. Easing their way across Pithlyn Mass, they swooped the talented, trained, aggressive, and those who desire to fight for Pithlyn pride, leaving behind the women, timid, and young.

As the motion expanded, the words jumbled like an elementary telephone line. By the time leading authoritators reached their fourth village, men believed King Avar had given word that he's ready to take over the entire sphere after reeling Glaci North and Zyder to his side. No thought of Makail's aggressive intrusion existed. Every word revolved around King Avar's lack of scruples and his hunger for ultimate power. Gossip even began regarding King Avar bribing the gargentwans to fight with him and, by the beginning of his rule over the entire sphere, deeming the gargentwans as superior beings under the gods.

While the three initial authoritators continued to work to the end of their wicks organizing a massive clan, Queen Bidellia spoke to her men who lined the rock steps ready to mount the raxars flexed just outside the large stable. "Our rival haunts our east, much like the past, but we've prepared for them with haste and vim." While pausing between words, Queen Bidellia paced on the grass beneath her castle with her geared up raxar tongue-splashing the stream behind her with Fidelis's and Dux's raxars quenching their equal morning thirst. Nearly one hundred committee members and guards listened closely to their queen's announcements ahead of the voyage to battle. "Now for this final time we stand amassed, I'll say that even if our hope is grim, we can't back down; defending Pithlyn Mass is most of all to all of those alive. We'll fight with vigor, love, and souls of brass, and gods above will see our Pithlyn thrive.

"The gargentwans will bring their bladed spheres while Zyder always has their throwing pierce; we know Dymetrice arms themselves with spears. A massive squall, but we will keep it fierce, as this attack will forge Endefder first, so we will fight with gods; our foe is cursed."

With her final word, Queen Bidellia turned toward Lady Leadtheway. Fidelis walked steadily behind his queen and watched her latch on the white raxar, scissor kicking into the saddle. Without hesitating, she used her foot to pounce her raxar's belly, and she dashed while Fidelis still tried to climb aboard his own raxar. Seeing the queen in such a hurry caused him to feel rushed and therefore clumsy, for he typically mounted a raxar with no such difficulty, but on this day, his ability resembled a neophyte, especially next to Dux who'd jumped atop his with ease and said, "Must I wait for such scattered inaptitude?" which only caused a more jittery man, telling Dux to close it. Eventually, Fidelis found the saddle with his rear, and the two darted through the stream, pursuing Bidellia with no chance of catching her. In the beginning of a battle, when traveling all the way across the mass, the concern lacked unity. Queen Bidellia held no importance in sticking together since they all aimed for the same resting points. The entire group would catch her by nightfall.

The drove of men filling the steps had raised their arms and roared, signifying enthusiasm for defending Pithlyn, ready to ride toward the rising sun with Queen

Bidellia leading her team. From Pithlyn Palace, they forged directly toward the village where all of her thousands of warriors would eventually meet prior to herding through to Endefder. Fiwel rested merely miles west of the healing flowers Gonko had once shown Makail. The queen, with her men, would wait in Fiwel until the other three immense troops arrived. Once the thousands of battlers all gathered around the proximity of Fiwel, Queen Bidellia would stand above them all to wage their blessings and conquer all for love of Pithlyn. However, many sunrises separated her from the point of Fiwel, as her league would travel a few thousand miles before arriving there.

From the cellar of Pithlyn's Palace, Makail could hear the clobbing hooves beat against Pithlyn soil. But with the guards' glares directed primarily on him, he could do nothing. The others in the confinary looked even more coarsely upon him, as impeding the progress of a royal party heeded hardly arbitrarily, to cause a battle with gargentwans permitted grounds for annihilation, although such a sentence could not be carried out except by the queen's order. Therefore his fate would rest until Queen Bidellia returned from battle.

For now, Makail had to continue on with the duties of an illmate. Today, falling in order, the group of thirteen had to straighten up the throne room. Since many committee members and guards had trampled through the room, leading to the main entrance, tidying begged. While eliminating a pest's nest in a crevice of the room's south mountain wall, Makail's thoughts revolved around fighting for Pithlyn, dreaming of fighting at Bidellia's side to defeat any beast against her.

Through his dreamlike thoughts, he saw Cil scraping at the same wall as him. Makail slid closer to Cil only to ask, "This battle, how long would it take this morning's fleet to reach the eastern border?"

"Why should I mention any bit of that to a traitor?"

Fury built up inside him, while keeping outward composure. "I am not a traitor," with a stern whisper, "I came to Pithlyn seeking the queen's hand, and I held it for a night, but then all this for coming here? It's absurd. I never thought it would come to this. Because it has, I must understand the queen's warpath."

"I will not speak of anything with you."

Annoyed, Makail threw himself back to the infested crevice, thinking of words to break through Cil. If he could get anybody to turn friendly towards him again, it'd be Cil. Mulling through ideas, he could only think of forcefully convincing Cil, yet he knew that wouldn't gain a friendly discussion. Makail had to make Cil believe him, for Makail had to know the duration of Queen Bidellia's journey.

By nightfall, as expected, the hoard of men had met with the queen in an average sized village called Hudwol. The women of this village were uncertain of the exact circumstances, so Fidelis and Dux honored the liberty of explaining everything to the authoritator's wife while skimming through the key notes with any other inquisitive mouth. By the hush of the village, Queen Bidellia slept on a kush in the same hut as Fidelis, who shuffled his blanket and exclaimed with grunts and sighs. Sensing exaggerated agitation of actions, she asked, "Oh, what's the worry of your mind tonight?" Without giving him time to answer, she explained, "We've passed this pathway not for days but one."

"That coward, worthless scum of a man! All this because of him! And you..." he scowled. Rarely did Fidelis exhibit any sort of emotion toward the queen, so when he did, something had really caused his boil. She never took it personally, understanding every soul occasionally needs to rid the fumes, saving purity, and with her being almost the only person to whom he ever spoke, she knew she would receive his hot air. "You steadied to collapse your graces for him! I could see the pain in your eyes, the disbelief. For a coward!"

Her next words, threw him aloof. He lost his grip and felt a pang inside as if Makail had been sorely misjudged, yet all of him wanted to believe his own conclusions.

She'd said to him, "I'd call Makail to ride with us and fight, for he's of gods." His blank stare urged Bidellia's ensuing words, "Isnelle and Jivin's son"

After moments of bewilderment, he scorned, "And they proved traitor too! Leaving Pithlyn for Dymetrice to enhance an opportunity for peace. HA! If that were true, then why would the next time they show a sign of themselves be in the form of their son who's instigated war between their new home and Pithlyn? They turned against us and their wretched son has been raised the same."

Politely considering his rebuttal, the queen closed for the night with, "On what a whim, we've weld him with the walls."

"Yes…where he certainly should be."

Assuming all flowed smoothly, by the time day one of the royal party's voyage closed, Pithly had already traveled around the Lake of Pithlyn with about twenty-five hundred men on track with Soren, plus a splitoff group pulling fighters from villages along the southern edge of Pithlyn Mass; Vafarm waited for north and south splitoffs in a village immediately west of the center bridge over the Pithlyn River, which they'd cross as a clan of more than three thousand; and due to their initial northward trail and waiting for a splitoff to round the mountains, Nearo's team lagged a couple days shy of crossing the Pithlyn River, passaging the northern bridge.

As the queen awoke for day two of this war's expedition, her fighting spirit rumbled within, immensely feeling a fierce threat against her beloved Pithlyn. She stepped from the hut—as the rest of the village continued to dream—towards Lady Leadtheway while grasping certainty of the battle ahead presenting a great struggle for her loyal arms. Gargentwans teamed with Dymetrice spears and potentially Zyder's pierce could equal too large a conquest for her men to overpower. Even with more than twenty thousand eventual men at Endefder's door, the gargentwans could barrel through them by the dozen.

Finding her raxar precisely where she'd left her, near a post at the end of a village path next to a large puddle of water, she grazed her palm along Lady's thick, muscular neck, saying, "It's you and I, my Lady Leadtheway." She untied Lady from the post and coiled the leash to rest it on the saddle's skirt. Kissing her under the eye, the queen swiped her legs to straddle the saddle, completing her chat, "So let us travel harsh while Omnerce calls." She absorbed great pride in leaving a village on a battle route with her royal league, but she also loved to gallop on Lady in the serenity of her open kingdom. Though it could seem eerie traveling along such vast land with forests, rivers, hills, and wild animals, but this was

Pithlyn under the rule of Living Goddess Bidellia.

She rode alone for the entire second day. Fidelis, Dux, and the rest of the pack never came within her seldom back glances, which could view miles in any direction with flat and open terrain during this segment. Primarily, the queen kept her focus on the foe. How to defeat them? How to restrain the gargentwans? How to convince King Avar to retreat and come to a compromise? She had no answer. King Avar had proven the most stubborn and convoluted king Dymetrice had ever crowned. His priorities pinched the opposite end of the spectrum from Bidellia's. He wanted absolute power without a care for whom he'd need to trample en route to achieving it; Queen Bidellia held the sought power, freely spreading it to all those of her mass and beyond.

In Dymetrice, King Avar had assembled twelve men from his castle to stroll with him down to their docks on the southern coast, which collides with the Simmery Deep. King Avar had hopped on his eternally black raxar, Gusto, to ride the four-day journey. The pursuing twelve men would foot the journey, carrying a few battle weapons and sacks of snacks. In woods just north of his castle, Tyban's enthused pack had rushed back to their ships parked in the Gelid Deep. By the time King Avar had reached his docks, two gargentwan ships had begun their journey to Dymetrice Point's water level, which would still take several days. With King Avar's need to stop his ships and acquire more fighters along the coast, the gargentwan's head start only meant they would wait longer for Dymetrian ships. And as Queen Bidellia neared her second village in the string to Fiwel, King Avar slept for his first night on a ship collecting men for battle.

A village called Queggor waited for the queen's arrival, as the village would provide the royal party's resting quarters after their second day of journeying. Queen Bidellia slowed Lady's pace leading into the village, and six women of Queggor received the queen before the edge of the dirt path, serving as the main entry to the village. These women held their right hands over their hearts to show respect and appreciation for their queen. Bidellia rode in quietly, acknowledging each woman with her head, and reaching out her hand for their embrace.

The final lady to touch Bidellia's hand was the authoritator's wife, Fye, who said respectfully, "I can take you to your hut for the night, my queen."

Bidellia angled her head to give an agreeing nod, and she followed. Typically the queen liked to interact with her people, every citizen inside Pithlyn Mass knew that. However, when she'd tread a trail toward battle, everybody knew not to disturb her, as her mindset would tend to give less conversation and more thought to strategy. So all evening, the queen stood in the same hut to which Fye had led her, thinking of her mind's past six days, wanting to lie down and fall asleep.

A couple hours passed for the queen to think quietly within the hut when Fidelis and the rest of the men began to file through the paths of Queggor. Fye and the other five ladies kindly showed each man to his hut for the evening, but when Fidelis was shown his, he declined, "I will sleep in the same hut as my queen." Confused, the lady took him to Fye, who recognized, "Of course, Fidelis is her most trusted man. We should have thought to keep them together for the night." Turning her attention to Fidelis, she instructed, "Follow me good sir."

Inside Queen Bidellia's hut, she silently, calmly paced between the two beds from head to foot. Fidelis watched from the doorway; her mind obviously lingered three thousand miles away, for she hadn't noticed his presence. When he said, "I'm glad to see you made it safely on your own, never doubted you would," she had no response and did not acknowledge the sounds. Her deep focus caused Fidelis to step to her, trying to hitch her attention without startling her. He cleared his throat, and she continued to pace, as if possessed. Finally, while the queen paced toward him, he said firmly, "My queen, your thoughts are struggling you." She stopped.

"I had some thoughts of my own during today's ride." Her expression allowed for him to go on, "Isnelle and Jivin, they did serve well; they served mighty. They were good to us and vowed for only good things to come of Pithlyn Mass. They may have raised this son of theirs to be a good man, and protect their motherland by the time he's of his current age. So it's possible that your most recent illmate has come here to protect our land."

The queen glared at him with narrow eyes. "You're better not to let your judgment sway," she warned.

"You're right. I apologize, my queen. He is a wretched man."

Momentum

On the third day after Queen Bidellia's departure from her castle, Makail kept persistence with Cil in trying to determine how much time remained before the Pithlyn army would clash with King Avar's men. Cil never uttered another word to Makail after saying so while cleaning the throne room. Agitated by Cil's silence, Makail knew he'd need to give a few details of himself in order to get his point across.

Because the queen and all of Pithlyn courted war, a standard procedure of the castle was to barricade the windows and prepare for quick security of doors, thus fastening door-length locks that would clamp across the door near the top and at eye level. Though unlikely for the battle to carry through all of Pithlyn and reach the castle, they must prepare for even the slimmest of chances. On this third day after Bidellia's departure, the illmates were assigned to this miscellaneous task.

As all the illmates worked on preparing the castle, Makail finished armoring his assigned window and noticed Cil and a frail illmate, Frisho, working on the front door's massive latch. Feeling the guard's glares, Makail calmly strutted along the throne room's east wall to provide assistance to Cil. Once he stood next to the two, he told Frisho, "You may not have strength enough for this task. I will finish this with Cil."

"I need your knowing words," directing his attention to Cil after Frisho walked off to find another portion of the castle to secure.

Cil said nothing, continuing to set the scaffold on a hinge just wide of the door's edge. These metal security clamps would sit in an upright position beside the door. The hinge allowed for the twin beam on the outside of the door to collapse in unison with the one on the inside. Catching these metal beams—fastened to the wall on the opposite edge of the door—were simple, sturdy metal L pieces. Enough potential intruder with enough men could lift the outer beam, which was why they'd constructed it with a removable hinge. This would cause the intruding to believe they'd unlocked the door and could invade the castle when really the door remained locked.

"Cil, my parents passed on to me their gifts of the gods, their strength of the gods. The gods had shone on my parents, and now, it's my turn to shine for the gods, as my strength exceeds what my parents once possessed combined." Cil acted as though he couldn't hear Makail. "I'm telling you, I have the power to save Pithlyn in this battle."

Cil broke his silence, "All you've had the power to do is begin this battle."

"My intentions have been misinterpreted, and I regret the corollary." "All I'm asking you is how long before the queen arrives in Endefder? On my travels to this place, I stopped in Endefder and spoke with a man named Gonko. He told me it takes the queen more than twenty days to travel out there. Is that accurate?"

Cil remained quiet, and Makail's mind reeled through what he should say next. As they came within minutes of finishing the door, Cil stated, "By the end of the thirteenth day, her drove will reach Fiwell, where they will meet with the other three enormous clans. Together on the fourteenth day, all twenty thousand or so in her band will storm to Endefder ready to protect." With his face growing stern, he added, "If you have any unworthy intentions with my words, I will have no part of it. You will not accuse me as a contributor, for everybody in here, plus the queen and her committee, would believe my word to yours." He paused for a moment, finishing hesitantly, "Yet, for some inexplicable reason, I believe in your righteousness."

"Thank you, Cil. I will use your shared knowledge with great honor." They finished attaching the beams on the upper and lower sections of the main door then practiced with a few trial runs, making sure the locks worked without flaws. By lunch, Makail had already begun planning an escape; he had nine days before he'd begin executing his plan.

On the third day after Queen Bidellia's departure from her castle, she left Queggor with her royal league immediately behind her and Fidelis and Dux to her sides, drafting slightly to the rear of Lady Leadtheway. All three of her splitoffs and splinters had clearly made it past Pithlyn's River or, in Soren's case, well beyond circling the Lake of Pithlyn. The flock of men rode the current of this wave fiercely, obtaining more and more fighters by the day. Queen Bidellia grew confident in their quest, knowing her numbers should outlast anything King Avar could bring to battle. Her forces could outnumber the gargentwans in a battle by twenty to one, allowing for her men to defeat such a disdained opposition.

As the wave continued to build momentum and strength throughout its push across Pithlyn soil, the queen realized how to confront King Avar. Her numbers would be the driving force for a compromise. King Avar could rest at ease with Queen Bidellia's offer to never reap havoc against his mass, if he'd remain tranquil toward hers. Otherwise, she has enough willing men to fight for her, not even including what she could bring with the involvement of Favally and Indiffron too. His cowardly fear would have to overcome him, causing him to retreat his men.

Days and days passed. Nearo, Vafarm, and Pithly had collected an incredible amount of men, and everybody remained on schedule. On the mass of Pithlyn, few dangers rested. Wild, untamed animals played the greatest, most intimidating obstacle, but whenever one attacked, plenty other men made sure the beast became their next meal and not the other way around. No great impediments existed, and never could any amount of rain or wind delay the course of these four thundering clusters. And now, by the end of tomorrow's travels, every cluster would meet at Fiwell where Queen Bidellia anticipated the largest battle turnout of her reign.

Makail awoke on the thirteenth morning, knowing, according to Cil, the queen and her entire Pithlyn army would reach Fiwell tonight. Therefore, he had to shove his plan into motion. Considering the stark criticism he'd received on a daily basis since returning to the confinary, his plan seemed reasonable. Most gave him the cold shoulder, like Cil, but Hanz, Grudon, and Wulym tormented and threatened him. Even a prisoner has great love and pride for their Pithlyn Mass. On one of the hunting days after the illmates had been released into the woods, Wulym even went so far as to hold his hunting spear to Makail's neck, saying, "If any of my friends die out their because of you, I will make sure you take your last breath."

During breakfast this day, Makail leaned against the dark door, which led to the unoccupied obscurium. He faced the empty cells, ignoring all other illmates to his right. When Hanz's voice rose above all else, however, Makail heard him say, "We should send him out so that the battle he started can finish him." Though Makail gave no reaction, Hanz laughed with Grudon and Wulym.

Still chuckling, Wulym began strolling toward Makail, leveraging, "But such a coward, I'm sure," looking back to Hanz with a smile, "would rather sit in here quietly while good Pithlyn men fight to subdue what he started." Wulym now stood between Makail and the empty cells without a plate in hand, as he'd already scarfed down his breakfast. Makail had half a plate left, but with thrilled bumps running up his torso and over his arms, he let the plate smack to the floor. The hazing and ridicule had become too much for him, and he could not take another antagonizing remark. His heart pounded while his mouth became tight and fierce. He had no handle on his next actions, as his emotions overflowed.

Chapter 19

Before his plate hit the ground Wulym's back cracked three cinder blocks between two cell doors; Makail had shoved his right hand directly into his chest. Wulym's feet hadn't even hit the ground, and Makail landed punch after punch on each cheek as fast as a piston shoots under the hood of a car. A final blow blasted the center of his forehead, crashing his head back to the blocks. Three guards gripped Makail before any more damage could be managed, grabbing his arms and shoulders.

"To the obscurium," one guard announced while another added, "which is where he should have been all along! Why the queen would rule against the obscurium, I may never understand."

Wulym attempted to shake away the pummeling but could hardly squint his eyes open to see a blurry, wobbly confinary. All of Wulym's pain flared through his back and face, for the initial shot to the chest left no semblance of a sore. Noticing the eyes partially open, Makail knew he had his attention, and reminded, "Unless I'm the one to spend the days in there."

With a mouth slobbering of blood, Wulym woozily declared, "You better hope you never get out of there!"

Leaning his head forward as the guards slid him through the door, Makail replied, "I can't wait to get out of here." Turning his attention to the guards before they shut the door, he asked, "Might I finish my breakfast in here?"

A bold and intimidating voice said, "After the rest have finished lunch, we'll slap a few bites to your floor. Unless they eat everything."

As the door slammed shut, Makail tried, "But I didn't gather enough energy from breakfast." The door had shut, and the blackness of an endless train tunnel filled his eyes, yet he continued complaining, "He came up to me with wrong words, and you punish me because I can stand my ground?" His voice quieted, as he began to think aloud, "I'm so misunderstood around here. Why won't people believe in me?

"They weren't kidding, it is impossibly black in here," Makail whispered to himself. "I can't even see my fingers while I touch my nose."

The darkness of Makail's temporary confinement, however, did not block out the sound. He could hear feet shuffling along the floor, guards speaking with illmates and shouting orders of what the agenda holds, and he could hear everybody file from the castle's confinary for the day's duty. Makail knew he was the only man left in the confinary, and with the agitating darkness compelling him to close his eyes, he hummed the tunes of the capisongs, easing his eyes to comfort. As the tune flowed from his soul, he sang the words he'd sung for Bidellia many days ago, except he switched his final line, singing,

"Oh when her beauty sees my eyes again, I'll thump the foe to see our Pithlyn win." His desire to battle for Pithlyn ran deeper than ever; his craving to dislodge the man responsible for his parents' deaths fueled his fighting spirit; his yearning to prove love for Pithlyn Mass captured his soul.

Earlier in the morning, the queen awoke, understanding the day's destination where some twenty thousand men would surround her ready for battle, expecting the ugliest foe. On this morning, considering the escalation of the day, she waited for her league and traveled out with Fidelis and Dux near her side. Not far from the gates of Village, she reminded her two near men, "Tonight we meet as one for glory's sake."

"Yes, my queen, for glory," Fidelis remarked.

"Yes, my queen," Dux began, "and tomorrow we slaughter all. Could a day ever be more wholesome than what's to come?"

Fidelis shook his head in near disgust of the comment, but the queen maintained her stiff composure. The greatest thirst Dux ever endured involved battling, for he carried, thrust, and steered his sword better than any man he'd come across. His mouth watered at the thought of fighting; it was almost a selfish ploy, whereas Fidelis viewed these battles as an act of love for mass; he assisted in the defense of his land when his land could not defend herself.   The queen knew Dux would fight honorably, ending with good deeds to her Pithlyn. Even if Dux's motivation ran foul, the outcome could not be matched by any of her other warriors, and she appreciated his enthusiasm.

On the other side, with this morning's sun rising on their backs, the gargentwans' two ships aimed directly at the Pithlyn coast with four massive Dymetrice ships closely trailing. Three trained gantors circled the ships from above with their trainers riding them armed with the newest of Dymetrice weaponry, zipping rings, created specifically for those steadying in flight—a flat steel blade, shaped and sized like a two-dimensional donut with sharp edges.

After traveling a couple hundred miles in this order, the ships had carried enough momentum to reach the shore in the same afternoon Queen Bidellia would reach Fiwel. Once the ships hit Pithlyn's coast, King Avar could continue his mission to hit an unexpecting Endefder first.

The Crest

As the slowly sloshing waves thinned, the gargentwans ships carved through Pithlyn's dampened coastline with King Avar's fleet next to slice the sandy surface. As King Avar's ship came to a halt, he peered north, figuring to have landed plenty south of the Pithlyn Wall. His crew sailed in a couple hundred miles south of Pithlyn Point, well out of sight and hearing range. Upon stoppage, all fighters emptied their vessels to receive command.

A warm mist filled the late afternoon air while those ready for war filed onto Pithlyn soil under slender gray clouds covering the entire sky. Gargentwans and loyal Dymetrice fighters let sand smush against their feet, lining the beach with gargentwans in the back—closest to the water. Down the center of the army, they'd formed an aisle for King Avar to ride his raxar from his ship, down the ramp, and dash to the front. Everybody awaited the king's announcement of directive, eager to fight, eager to overtake Pithlyn. Once all his men were set appropriately, King Avar hopped atop his raxar and thudded down the ship's ramp. Quietly, quickly, sand tossed from under his raxar's steps as King Avar made his way to the front.

"Our journey thus far has been no more than a deep breath, so let us breathe easy tonight. We shall board our ships once more and rest. Before sunrise, our energies will have gathered enough to prowl through this land and take it over completely." Without waiting to hear a response from his gallery, King Avar, tapped his raxar and returned to his ship.

Late in the evening, Makail awoke from his afternoon slumber in the blackest chamber the sphere could offer. He could hear the tinkering of guards locking all the cage doors for each illmate, while telling them not to speak another word for the night. Once all the cages had been locked, and aside from the faint voices of guards speaking quietly, Makail could only hear silence, so he began to envision his plan. The second part of his plan appeared simple enough, for he'd felt the north wall of his new chamber earlier in the day. As he expected, the wall had the same surface as his former cell. The mountain. With rubble clattering to the ground, however, the noise could rattle the guards, so he had to wait until the snores of many reverberated through the confinary. Loud sleepers would surely drown out his racket.

He didn't have to wait long. The guards voices could not even be heard over the lawnmower snores of what sounded like every illmate in the confinary. Makail turned to the mountain wall and, in the lower right corner, rubbed his hand along the rocky surface. Like a god, he steadied his hand above the wall and caused the mountain crumbs to crumble onto the floor of the obscurium. Due to his blindness for this endeavor, he made the grinding gravel cease so he could feel the depth of the hole he intended to create. Then he allowed the wall to trickle into smithereens. He continued with this on and off until he could feel a deep enough start to his tunnel. By then, the pile of mountain dust had built as tall as himself, but he could snuggly lie his entire body in the tunnel. As he continued to turn the inside of this mountain into debris, he brushed the loose stones behind him, keeping his path clear.

From spending many days fulfilling illmate duties on the outside of the castle, Makail had a measurement of where he needed to direct his trail. His initial movement, as he'd already begun, led him a short distance downward into the mountain further under the castle's lowest floor—the confinary. His quickest exit after a deep enough dig, would advise him to angle his progress to run parallel with sea level, which would also allow for an easier task of keeping the debris away from where he needed to continue pathing. Since the pebbles he'd just dismantled would skitter back toward him, they served as a perfect indicator for how level his path was becoming once he began to veer the tunnel straighter.

Along a flat tunnel, his forethought plan would carry through with ease. Despite a lack of extra space as he slinked down his path, he'd crumble the mountain, swipe the debris, crumble, swipe, crumble, swipe, crumble, swipe, repeatedly for what seemed like the entire night. Makail hadn't realized how far set back the castle was compared to the mountain wall. He thought it would last as a quick task, but he continued on, hoping to sniff the open air soon. With his focus keen on this repetition, he crumbled, swiped, and looked to crumble again when he noticed a small hole to Pithlyn air. The crumbling halted as he exhaled deeply. At last, he thought as relief settled. With a final hand burst, pebbles bounced down the mountain wall, and Makail had his opening.

After climbing from his hole, the mountain's surface, though slightly steep, was walkable. And he walked all the way to the base, just to the north of where he and Bidellia had had their dual. Makail looked back to the castle as it glistened golden peaks against the midnight sky. Before turning toward his own battle trail, he said aloud, "Yup, couldn't wait to get out of there." Then he dashed, not to meet with the queen and all others at Fiwell, but to meet Gonko in Endefder so he could wait there while the queen and her men strolled in. Makail knew this run would take all night, just as it had some forty nights ago when he scorched from Endefder to the western coast.

Before Makail had begun his trail from the obscurium, across the mass, a colossal flock exceeding twenty thousand men engulfed the village of Fiwell. Leagues of men spread in every direction as Queen Bidellia's troops arrived to applauding men. Yes, these men were ready to protect their Pithlyn, Bidellia's Pithlyn, and the queen knew such a turnout necessitated an address. First, however, she and Fidelis were shown to the authoritators dwelling, where the two of them would sleep for the night. Once everything had settled, she remounted Lady Leadtheway and galloped through the village, without Fidelis, toward her army. Directing her raxar, she rode out to the village limits, and circled the village, which allowed for her to view the first row of men who'd come to battle. Slowing her raxar, she stepped her through the men, as each would dodge and bow as she came near, clearing her path just in time. Once through, she circled the perimeter of her army, a much longer ride than her first circle. Sizing up her man count, she prepared a few words in her head.

Lady swayed back to the center of the village, and Queen Bidellia rose from her saddle and stood where her butt had tapped most of the past thirteen days. She stood very tall atop her raxar, and she directed her voice to the gods, for she needed the gods to catch her words and reverberate them back as her most stentorian voice. "Attention," she began as her voice boomed off Gracen loud enough for every man around Fiwell to hear it clearly. "Thank you all for coming here and standing ready to protect our mass. Tomorrow, we will set aside the fear to fight with courage, letting no man pass!" Her voice was like a cannon in echo. She spoke with poise toward Gracen, and Gracen sent the words down with elegant thunder. "We stand tonight with twenty thousand strong; we fight so soon with strength of all behind, and gods will bless our battle cries with song, defeating foe while fighting intertwined with gods who'll lead us to a gloried end. So rest tonight, obtain your strength to fight."

Fidelis had heard his queen speaking, and rushed from their quarters, not even taking the time to drop his sword. He watched from behind her as she'd held both her arms apart and her head back, as if she meant to feel rain on this dry evening. Once she finished, she turned her feet and dropped to straddle Lady. With sounds of excited cheers enveloping them, she noticed Fidelis's presence and sword. As Lady strutted past Fidelis, the queen hushly mentioned, "You must be glad he had a sword to lend."

Looking down to the sword, he proclaimed, "I thought I'd grabbed mine," he began to walk shortly behind his queen, while voicing enough for her to hear, "but noticed it was his after we'd already begun our journey."

"You need not lie; this sword should serve you right. We'll pray it has a fighter's soul entrenched."

"I'll become its fighting soul, for there's been no more righteous man to carry such a described sword than me!" Fidelis declared.

Queen Bidellia gave Fidelis no response, allowing him to feel truth in his own words, which satisfied him. Their quarters for the night were on the way to where Bidellia would tie her raxar, so Fidelis stepped aside when they began to cross the door where he would wait for her to return. However, by the time the queen returned, Fidelis had already fallen asleep on a narrow grass-cushioned plank.

On the Carné Coast, a breeze chilled the air, and King Avar awoke with early-morning shivers. Within his ship, his highest men slept in a room adjacent to his. So as he trembled, he slowly stepped to his door, shaking the handle before pulling it to him. Staggering to the next room, he entered, clunking his sword against the floor until he heard movement from all twelve men. With a quivering jaw and a weary mouth, King Avar commanded, "W-w-wake them a-all. This is—our ti-time!"

The twelve men paired off and knocked on everybody's door throughout the six ships, including the gargentwans. As fighters awoke, the king's men directed them to line up on the coast as they had last night. Dymetrians understood the urgency of this command given the circumstances. This morning called for no time to lollygag; this morning allowed for no weak or weary souls; the strong came—the strong must show up.

While his men roused his army, King Avar centered his mind on taking Pithlyn, sharpening his senses, preparing to give his best, for this, he felt, would be the battle this sphere would never forget. He'd become a hero to his motherland, and a godlike being to all others for all of time. This battle would transform his reign from malcontent to unforgettably legendary. King Avar gave himself a look through. His boots, his battle attire, his sword, his shield—he was ready. "Our time!" he shouted to no one as he walked through his door to find Gusto.

The first ray of morning light had not pierced the sky when he jumped atop his raxar and hooved down the ramp. His army anticipated his entrance on the shoreline with swords drawn, indicating their own zest for battle. As Gusto hit the sand, King Avar halted him to admire his loyal followers. His pride sated his soul, and he knew the forthcoming battle would hold epic measures. Gusto, on his master's command, charged down the center aisle, breaking with a 180-degree spin on his hind legs.

"This morning men," the king announced, "we exhale our deep breath with a whale! Let them hear you all through Pithlyn. Let them know we've come to win, and we will leave no man standing until the battle is ours."

With the aisle still open between the bellowing fighters, King Avar called, "Gargentwans, come forth. You will lead behind me to encounter the adversary first."

Following command, every gargentwan gaped with long strides to the front, and they would walk before the Dymetrice men, serving primarily as protection, and to start the battle with a real throttle. The king led, which was purely customary, for turning one's back to royalty displayed one of the highest forms of disrespect, unless ordered to do so.

Once the entire herd of gargentwans stood before him, King Avar finished with his sword raised, "Let us

storm this maddening mass and flex are strength on all!"
He slowly turned his raxar to head deeper into Pithlyn
territory with the enthusiastic barks of his men following
him into the kingdom of the one and only Living
Goddess.

King Avar kept a steady stroll on his raxar to not pull
far ahead of his followers, for they all made this crusade
by foot. As a riotous pack ready to slay, they jaunted
over rolling hills of deep-green and very tall grass. The
thin cloud cover from last night had scattered, leaving
nothing throughout the dark blue, predawn sky. And the
mouths of one hundred and fifty gargentwans began to
soak themselves, anxious for revenge.

Makail's blazing journey continued furiously. He'd
shot across the four-mile bridge of Pithlyn River and
bumped through the rolling hills immediately following
the water. His mind remained keen on protecting Pithlyn
with a greater spirit than any other fighter's ever had,
holding nothing back, revealing everything, avenging his
parents' deaths. As his thoughts circled around the
ensuing battle with building animosity, his lightning pace
quickened. But with King Avar on the move directly
toward Endefder, even Makail could not run fast enough
to save the village.

C r a s b

From the moment Makail turned his back to Queen Bidellia's castle, he ran. He never looked back again, only forward. He never paused to catch a breath, or allowed for any hindrance in his pace; he ran straight, across the southern bridge, and through the rolling hills; he didn't care if a night owl spotted his insane speed. Makail bolted through Pithlyn faster than he had many days ago from Endefder to Pithlyn's Palace. He owned one purpose: find his queen to prove his love for Pithlyn Mass.

Just before the sun began its daily ascent from the eastern horizon, King Avar could see a small village ahead of him to the north as he stooped atop the western most foothill of the region. He turned to Tyban, who'd followed at the king's prompt right, "Wait here." He steered Gusto to reverse direction and coursed diagonally toward his following legion, aiming to meet before his southernmost fighter. The dash raced his raxar primarily downhill, as the rest of his army still descended from the previous hill. Before they reached the basin, King Avar had attained the southern boundary of his men. Facing Gusto north, he clucked the raxar's fierce belly, causing him to bolt in front of Dymetrice fighters.

Seeing their king cross before them, every member of the pack knew to halt his progress. He turned Gusto back south after he'd found his northernmost line. Slowly, the king strutted his raxar back south as his men stopped before crossing the threshold Gusto had created. "Ayon this next hill rests a village." He spoke loud enough for those still descending on the hill to hear him, knowing not everybody in the line would manage to hear every word. "A village of worthless Pithlyn varmint. This village contains the first of souls sacrificed by their queen before she surrenders to our forces. We will leave little in this village, but first, two of our gargentwans will visit the people, and we shall await their call. This means hold back until we hear the roar of the gargentwan! Hold back until the gargentwans roar!" he repeated up and down the line, making sure everybody understood the battle plan.

With his army completely static, King Avar rode back to his gargentwans, finding Tyban and Junder in the front line of giant warriors. He steered Gusto in front of the two, and even on his raxar, King Avar eyes did not set higher than their waists. He called up to them, "You two started this," nabbing their attention. "It will be the two of you to walk alone into this village they call Endefder. You will ask one man if they've seen the man who pummeled you two." At his words, a gargantuan fury boiled within the two gargentwans. "When the man says he's never seen a man of your description, you [pointing at Tyban] call him a liar and roar as loudly as you ever have. On your roar, my legion will rage in to slaughter the entire village."

"We will!" Tyban agreed. Junder matched his stride as they marched directly toward the village.

As they quickly approached the village with their long steps, Tyban told Junder, "This is how we make things right. This is what we must do to save our name. The gargentwans are never crossed!" Junder already understood the significance of this battle and nodded his head in agreement.

Typically, Gonko was the first to rise in Endefder, and this morning served no difference. From fifty yards away, Gonko could see the two human monsters walking toward his village. The two were obviously gargentwans, for no beast appeared so human except in stature. Gonko knew gargentwan loyalties rested with his queen, so curiosity piqued his early morning mind.

"Hello," Gonko called as they progressed closer, "Do you two bring a message for us?"

Neither answered, though Gonko knew each had attained hearing distance. Therefore, Gonko's curiosity altered to peculiarly concerned.

As Tyban stood immediately in front of Gonko, he never intended to answer the question. Instead, he asked, "Have you seen a man about this tall?" holding his hand halfway down his thigh. In his mind, Gonko flipped through the men in his village who would match the height designation, while also wondering why they sought a man. "He has good build for a short one. He may have had a mark here," raising his right arm and rubbing his side.

It clicked. Gonko said, "Yes, many mornings ago a man named Makail came to me. He is a good Pithlyn man. Why do you wish to find him?"

Tyban's breaths became shorter and deeper as his eyes bugged. "Where is he?" he thundered.

"Why he sought our queen, and I told him the way. It's a long journey from here, but he should have reached her by now."

"You let him go?" and he finished the question with the roar only gods can make, like a lion echoing his roar in a valley surrounded by mountains. King Avar's men had no trouble hearing the elongated boom, and the rest of the gargentwans charged with thousands of Dymetrice fighters behind, including the three on gantors.

Following the roar, Tyban took a baseball swing with his bladed sphere, striking an unexpecting Gonko across the head with its rod. Gonko flopped to the ground unconscious where he did not stay long, for Junder swooped him up with both hands, raised him over his head, and then heaved him over the first and second line of dwellings onto the dirt path inside the village.

Every citizen of Endefder woke up to the deep, exploding resonance outside. When they came to find the disturbance, they saw gargentwan bile with a herd storming behind them. A few remained in the path next to Gonko's body, trying to wake him. His chest still pumped, so they knew he was alive, but he could not respond or open his eyes, not even for his beloved Biantha. But as Gonko coughed a dribble of blood, she irately turned, briskly moving back to their hut to grab Gonko's sword. When she came back to her husband, Tyban and Junder had already made it to him. She steadied the sword and aimed directly at Junder, screaming "Leave him alone!"

At her voice, Tyban turned, wailing his weapon toward the sound, and Biantha's course crossed gargentwan staff as the sphere rolled into her chest, breaking through skin and sternum, stopping her dead in her tracks, literally.

The gantors had reached Endefder before those by foot, and the men guiding the three enormous birds launched their circular blades like frisbees from above at any Pithlyn person visible. They only used their air attacks when not many, if any, from their own side invaded an area due to unreliable accuracy. And until the rest of King Avar's army stormed through the village, these men on gantors flung those blades furiously.

Endefder had no warning; they had no time to prepare or ready their weapons; the village scrambled for the weapons Queen Bidellia had graciously delivered so many years ago, trying to blockade this onslaught, but King Avar's men arrived quickly with a take-over mentality. Their spears worked to perfection as they could jab at men from a distance, tallying kills before meeting the range of a counterattack. Endefder had no chance against Dymetrice numbers combined with gargentwan strength. The gargentwans hurled bodies through the air like a shotput competition. The throwing of enemy bodies allowed the gargentwans to feel superior, in addition to being more entertaining. Dymetrice fighters had to search the village for fresh blood since the gargentwans had led the way and cleared most. But on this morning, the village of Endefder could not live up to a promise made to their queen, for not a single breath of Pithlyn souls exhaled within moments after King Avar arrived. The gargentwans did not take their time finishing the village, and Dymetrice men were thirsty for battle after not losing a single man.

Makail's progress blazed a trail heading mainly north, slightly east, three villages from Fiwel without a clue of the massacre in Endefder. His direction came from recalling his path to the castle. He remembered the distance and sensed the course necessary to find Fiwel, knowing it rested just west of the Flowers. On his line, he paced an angled straight shot to his destination.

Next in King Avar's line would be Fiwel, where Queen Bidellia awoke, startled by her late dream. With the knob of her sword, she unkindly nudged Fidelis, "We're under raid! No time for acting blenched!"

Weary, Fidelis questioned, "What do you mean, we're under raid?"

"They've hit Endefder!" she stated, while donning her queenly battle dress, which was no different than what she wore around her castle or on a stroll through Favally.

"How do you know, my queen," Fidelis had sat up, not quite standing yet.

"Omnerce speaks to me. You know my father never leads astray."

Dux, pleasantly agog, had stood just outside the queen's door, and he heard the conversation inside.

Unable to resist further, he opened the door. "You say we're fighting now!"

Both whipped their heads to the door, not expecting an eavesdropper. Fidelis sat speechless, so the queen spoke, noting Dux's credulous smile. "Yes," she whispered before heightening her voice, "such a battle though deserves no glee. Dymetrice looms..." she shifted her focus to a window left of Dux, "they've pounced to pound their prey."

"I will alert them all," he assured, rushing away from the queen's abode, ignoring the words advising him to calm down. He scurried through the village with great enthusiasm "This war has begun!" Up and down the Fiwell streets, he screamed, "They've hit Endefder! Let's go get 'em! Wake up, wake up, bad blood needs a shedding! Let's go!" He ran out to the myriad raxars resting with masters, as well as those who'd come completely by foot. "Get your weapons ready now! We fight in imminence. C'mon, saddle your raxar, there are men ready to find their afterlife!"

Every man Dux passed jumped to his feet and either slapped his face or dumped water over his head, if he had some reserved. Few awoke groggy this morning, for every man fell asleep knowing the trip to Endefder would likely end with a battle, but none of them expected this news from Dux.

Chapter 21

The queen rushed to her raxar, leaving Fidelis in the hut, still preparing, fumbling with unsteady haste. She wasted no time in commanding Lady to lead the way, as she clacked her hooves through the village with a vigor no other raxar possessed. As she crossed the waking Pithlyn legion just outside the village, Dux caught the white raxar galloping away, and he yanked his raxar to follow. Suddenly, a storm of hooves from Pithlyn raxars disrupted the tranquil grass, heading toward the Flowers. On the other side of those Flowers lay a narrow forest before the decimated village of Endefder.

In the narrow forest, unbeknownst to Queen Bidellia and her entire army, the Dymetrice league sought breakfast—even the gantors dove down with their masters for a meal—as the sun began to perch on the horizon, like the thumbnail of Omnerce. Continuing her approach, the queen's army gained ground with Dux closing the distance fastest. Before reaching the Flowers, she had Dux to her immediate right and an immense clan only a raxar-length or two behind her.

With so many men on raxars, the ground trembled for radial miles, and King Avar could feel their line of confrontation. The gargentwans could sense this ground quiver, as well, as it caused them to channel their heads west. King Avar glared toward Tyban, who'd accompanied the King for their breakfast hunt. "Why are they coming?"

Dumbfounded, he gandered, "This is their land. We are on their land."

"You fool! They have no business knowing of this invasion. How could they know!" Receiving a blank cheek, the King pried deeper, "Have you set me up, you overgrown behemoth? Did you plan this attack on me so Pithlyn could eternally silence me?"

"I did not. I came with you to avenge defiance."

"Fine. This only makes things trickier. Help me gather them all and form our battle lines. Breakfast will have to wait."

The two broke apart; Tyban gathered north and King Avar south. Most had felt the shuddering land and floated their eyes with curiosity as Tyban grudged through, bouldering, "Everybody get to the west of these woods. We must prepare for battle. We must defeat them all!" His voice caused a mixture of excitement and panic. Excited to taste a battle, panicked in wondering why Pithlyn came in force on their surprise attack.

To the south of Tyban after King Avar had shouted, "The battle has come to us now! Form our forces to the west of these woods, and let every part of Pithlyn feel our wrath," his people asked him, "What do you mean the battle has come to us? They shouldn't know of this."

King Avar responded simply, "Perhaps the gods

speak to the wrong aisle of royalty."

With arms folded across their protruding chests, Tyban and Junder stood on each side of King Avar on Gusto, as the three centered themselves on the front line. Each man in the line could see the boiling wave of milk chocolate flushing toward them surrounded by dirty clouds filling the brightening air. With this visibility, King Avar turned to his right and said, "Tyban, accept my apology for calling you an overgrown behemoth."

Tyban viewed the king, smiling, "I accept your apology," then Tyban patted the king's head.

Nobody pats the head of royalty. But what could King Avar do? "Great! Now let's finish our reason for coming here and conquer Pithlyn!" keeping the gargentwan's loyalties to him.

In the midst of soft brown raxars charging at Dymetrice army, Queen Bidellia's white raxar and multi-layered blue gown made her the overhanging ornament jutting from the rest. To the king, he could already smell her impenetrable skin, causing the pellets of sweat on his forehead to stream, his muscles to tense, and his nose to flare. His hatred grew with every further inch the queen's league advanced.

Just before her army trampled over Medeal's Flowers, Queen Bidellia, pulled the neck cords of Lady, slowing to a halt. As she slowed, Dux rushed past her and headed straight toward the throat of Dymetrice, which waited to swallow him. More Pithlyn raxars zoomed past the queen, and by raxar riders alone, the queen's league outnumber the king's. Yet, Medeal above knew this day would take all her strength.

Dux was first to clash with Dymetrice men, slipping under a swiping gargentwan arm, never slowing down, and as he quickly approached a line of Dymetrice born men, one hoisted his spear, poised to stab. Dux recognized this stance, drawing his sword with his left hand ready to defend the spear. With smearing speed, Dux anticipated the Dymetrice jab; blasting toward it, Dux swiped his sword beyond the spear's extended razor edge, slicing the weapon in two. His quick reflex backlashed his sword to the Dymetrice neck who tried spearing him off his raxar. Pulling his sword back to him, his raxar continued with terrorized speed, racing through the rows of Dymetrice fighters. In one row, two men with spears slipped their shields aside to better aim for Dux, ploying to strike him from each side by tossing their spears, but the raxar ran too fast, soaring past the two fighters before either spear could strike. The spears zipped right behind Dux, landing in the heart of the opposite thrower. Dux glanced behind him to see the two lying on the ground with a spear standing on top of each chest. He patted his raxar along the neck and said,

Chapter 21

"We'll call that three, big boy!"

As Dux reached the last layer of Dymetrice's army, nobody else could find as much success battling the gargentwans on the front line. These gargentwans possessed more than enough strength to snatch a charging raxar off the ground with both hands and slam the animal's back across their knee. After the knee blast, they would dump the raxar on top of its fallen rider, suffocating him. Sometimes, the gargentwans didn't even bother with the raxar and backhanded the rider to the ground.

King Avar never moved. He savored the witnessed destruction caused by his gargentwans and laughed at the fools crawling to the Flowers. He continuously glanced to the white and blue figure standing beyond the flowers, watching in horror. She stared back at him, noticing his pompous impression. She had to do something; she'd come to either fight or make peace without fighting. At the scene, her latter strategy was out.

The queen quickly reeled through her options and steered her raxar to a field of fallen Pithlynians. As Lady Leadtheway started her motion of the queen's guiding, Fidelis appeared at her side with Makail's sword in his holster. "My apologies in tardiness," he confessed.

She nodded her head and continued with Lady.

Surrender

"Your body ever rests with Pithlyn Mass, but Omnerce honors soul in Gracen's light." Queen Bidellia had dismounted Lady and stood over a recently killed fighter with her sword grazed against his chest. She performed this ritual to the first four beloved Pithlynians she crossed who had not made it to the Flowers before eternally closing their eyes. After the fourth time she blessed a fallen body, Fidelis had to interrupt: "My queen, I respect your words upon the bodies of our honored dead, but many more men battle to their own death right there. We must fight with them! You are the only one capable of chopping down a giant and ending any other challenger. We must fight with our league, my queen!"

Lost in her own puckering emotions of the battle she'd forced so many of her beloved people to fight, she could not fight herself. She did not have the audacity to allow this onslaught to continue and attempt to rectify the losses. She realized her attempt to bring as many men as she could translated to more lives sacrificed, and Queen Bidellia never sought a war bringing more pain and more loss, than resolve and gain. A Pyrrhic Victory is no victory at all. "This faulty fleeting flail of hope I had has caused the many deaths we see," shaking her head watching the stillness of a Pithlyn man she'd never met, who'd just lost his life for his love of Pithlyn Mass, "it's sad."

"It is sad, and we must make it right!" continuing to press his point.

While the queen hiked back up to her seat on Lady's back, essentially ignoring Fidelis's plea, Dux, off his raxar, battled the Dymetrice army from the back line, slashing through foe with great ease, and dodging spears with a kind of quickness no Dymetrice man could have anticipated. He voiced his smile with words like, "You can't move faster than that?" and "You couldn't use your spear with more authority?" and "Your shields are useless if you can't keep up with me!" Sliding past his raxar, intending for another swarm of Dymetrians, he called, "Twenty-two, big boy! Nobody poses a challenge here!"

Queen Bidellia, in contrast to Dux's attitude, hunted for King Avar, who stood on the fringe of Medeal's

Flowers where wounded Pithlyn fighters attempted to delay their final breath. With Fidelis following, she'd watched her army get throttled and thwarted enough and sought a word with the darkest king she'd known. He hadn't moved since the fighting began, so spotting him while riding for him served a simple task. On each side of him, Tyban and Junder only moved to wipe out any enemy aiming directly at the king. As the queen neared, Junder tilted down to ask, "Would you like us to keep her back?"

"I don't believe that will be necessary, but thank you."

In Fiwel, Makail walked through the empty paths, wondering where the massive army could be. He thought if Cil had led him astray, had Dymetrice already been through, or had the battle never taken place. Along the western boundary of Fiwel, just outside a row of huts, women stood behind children with their backs to the village. Makail walked between two huts then two women to view in the same direction. As he sidestepped through, the woman to his right said to the woman on her right, "I hear they've come with gargentwans all because King Avar wants to dominate all of Prodigion."

"It doesn't matter," the other lady responded. "Our queen will stop anybody for the protection of her people, her mass."

Chapter 22

The woman immediately to Makail's right snapped her head toward him. "No sword for a man with your physique?" "Why will you not fight for Pithlyn?"

Makail stared at her eyes then looked toward Medeal's Flowers hidden by thick woods. He could hear the faint echoes of battle song and realized this battle had begun. He had to stop it. As the women gasped in astonishment and the children jumped with excitement, Makail bolted with extreme heat.

With Lady's nose at a short distance in line with Gusto's, Queen Bidellia leaped to the ground. As Pithlyn forces ran into the wall of gargentwans, the battle besieged opposing royalty, and she waved her head north and south before facing King Avar, understanding the sore mistake she'd made. Her chin leaned up to the king, and she said, "I give you me, let Omnerce choose the rest." Her words never blinked, but when she began speaking, Makail blurred over Fidelis, yanking his sword from Fidelis's carrier in mid-air, flipping onto Queen Bidellia's saddle. As he sat, listening to the queen's words, his eyes wandered to disastrous surroundings. Gargentwans spinning raxars to the ground, bareback or not; blood crying from the mouth as a gargentwan fist finishes a Pithlynian; and spears peaking between gargentwan legs, spurring through enemy hearts. Makail's throat dried, for Pithlyn, despite the number,

246

stood no chance against a Dymetrice army led by gargentwans. The queen finished, "My Pithlyn vows surrender, ending drear."

Fidelis fumbled his lips, attempting to scorn Makail who should have been serving time in the castle's confinary, but nothing except small childish jabber escaped. On the other hand, captured by Bidellia's latest words, Makail used a sure mouth, defiantly announcing, "She lies." At the words, she diced her head around to see who made such impudent accusations on the Living Goddess. King Avar gaped his mouth, recognizing the perfect combination of Jivin and Isnelle. With her eyelids slipped to slits, she saw him. A rugged, dashing, bold, and daring man. She saw him. He was not like the others. His actions never resembled her as on a pedestal like the treatment she received from any other man to cross her. Yet, he revealed great respect for her and regarded her as though no other woman existed. And there he was; she saw him. A man who came to prove his love for her mass, their mass.

Never pausing in his words, Makail snarled his nose intensely, "I give you me as foe of quest," clearing his face, forming boisterous syllables, "for Pithlyn never will surrender here!"

The queen authoritatively marched back to her raxar with a maddened eye. Fidelis recognized her look of utter disdain, attempting, "My queen, I could not stop him! He flew in here like a gantor out of nowhere!"

She ignored Fidelis, and to the side of Lady, she peered up to Makail, softly declaring, "You'll fight for Pithlyn Pride with passion's best, as courage has become your former fear."

Tyban and Junder spoke quietly to King Avar, making him aware of the man on Queen Bidellia's raxar. "That is him. He is the one we are after." King Avar's eyes concentrated on the man across from him. Forehead, cheek, and mouth like Jivin; eyes, nose, and chin like Isnelle. "If he is why we've come all this way, destroy him. Leave no sign that he ever walked this sphere!"

Makail replied to his queen, "I'll fight with fear inside my beating chest, for fear of fears is losing you my dear," looking deeper in her oceanic eyes, "my love." He leaned down, pressing his lips against her forehead. "My love," he repeated, bringing his face away from hers and spinning off the saddle to avoid the immense forearm swiping over his head. "And they've come back for more!" he shouted, catapulting into the air, positioning to land on Tyban's back.

Watching him stream through the sky, she whispered, "My love."

As he landed on Tyban, Tyban shook like a wet dog,

only slower, trying to rattle Makail off his back. Makail's tense grip on the bulging trapezoids allowed him to steady his spot. Tyban flung his arms from side to side, continuing his efforts to release Makail, but Makail couldn't budge. Letting go of Tyban with his right hand, keeping the firm squeeze with his left, Makail chimed his sword and yelled, "For Pithlyn!" He fixated the sword to the sky, then hacked it back to propel it with maximum force into the neck of Tyban. Tyban arched his back, violently gasping for the breath he couldn't find, causing Makail to plop to the ground, slipping his sword down with him, leaving quickly oozing blood to gush down the gargentwans back and chest. Junder watched with amazed fear, stiffened, stifled; his wide eyes couldn't even blink.

Makail turned to King Avar, carrying a rocky tone, "You surrender now! Retreat!"

King Avar chuckled. "You took down a gargentwan all by yourself. You are the boy I expected. Therefore, you should know, I never enter anything to surrender before I have accomplished my mission. Your parents knew that very well," reverting to laughter.

Makail bolted into the king, "Then see my parents!" as he speared the king with his shoulder, driving the king to the ground while keeping his own feet. Turning, Makail grasped further thought on his own words and added with shrugging shoulders, "if it weren't for Core."

From the ground, King Avar bounced to his feet, for great humiliation came with royalty grounded. He turned to face Makail. "You imbecile! Nobody, and I mean nobody, attacks the Dymetrice King without submitting to the ultimate punishment. Now come, and I'll show you the path to your parents!"

Shaking his head with a smirk for the pathetically rapacious king, Makail said, "My kin would rather see you meet defeat." Not one second after the words left his mouth, he'd bolted to the south end of King Avar's battle line, where gargentwans mangled with raxars and men less than one-third their size.

On his departure, King Avar screamed "Coward! Come fight me. I will end you!"

Queen Bidellia marked the word, and declared, "He's not a coward; let him soar. He's merely trouncing forces to deplete your league."

The king took great aim at Bidellia. "You want more Pithlyn men to die. Keep to your surrender, or the only bloody flesh will reek of Pithlyn men."

The gargentwan on the far end peered down with a raxar in hand. He tossed the animal and leaned in to swipe Makail, intending to launch him through the air, but once his body flexed toward Makail, Makail began his instant rampage, pummeling up the line at his warp speed. As he blurred up this battle line, he tapped each gargentwan he crossed, like tipping trees in Quintix Valley, only he sent the gargentwans floating backwards, causing them to blast up, like water trailing a jetski. King Avar wrapped his head around to watch the peach wave arch over the trees. Astonished, he realized the excessive strength of this one individual, and he knew the only way now to win this battle would be to kill Makail.

As the monster-sized humans flopped and thudded to the ground, they'd smash on either trees or Dymetrice men who couldn't jump away quickly enough. Dux continued his masterous swordsmanship on the opposite side of the forest. As a narrow forest though, he could feel vibrations through his boots as the gargentwans landed nearly simultaneously for an extended period. Never hesitating with his swipes and blocks, Dux showed why many considered him the best mortal swordsman, yelling to his raxar, "Thirty-four!"

When Makail finished the entire line of gargentwans, Dymetrice fighters fought exposed, no longer able to hide behind the trunk legs of giants, making for a much fairer battle. However, Dymetrice still held greater wits on fighting, and gantors still hovered above with their riders picking off Pithlyn men at random. Allowing for King Avar to remain confident, despite the temporary fall of his near impenetrable front line, when Makail asked,

Chapter 22

"Surrender yet?" as he appeared in front of King Avar.

"Come die, Makail."

He tilted his head and dragged his lips up a cheek, stating, "I'd hate to end the one who took my parents' lives."

King Avar stood armed with a spear in his left hand and a king's sword in his right. "Despite how quickly you move, I will slash away until you no longer draw air."

Clinching his sword, Makail knew the gods would glimmer down on him for this fight, and he was ready to duel with his disgraceful former king. Makail stood firm, studying King Avar's slightest move when Junder grabbed him by the arm. The tight squeeze suffocated Makail's bicep, disenabling him to move. With his other arm free, grasping his sword, he swiped toward the thick wrist, causing Junder to release him. Makail knew if Junder handles a full grip on him, the duel would probably be over, as King Avar would joust his blade into an immobile Makail with ease. Still feeling as though Junder's hand held his arm, Makail circled with King Avar, essentially keeping a tight rope between them. King Avar inched their gap thinner and thinner until close enough to jab the spear toward Makail's heart. An easy whip of the sword knocked the spear off course, and as Makail's sword followed through, whistling by the king's right arm to blocked his sword.

Smirking at the king's inadequate attempts, Makail noted, "You'll never land."

"Close your lips and prepare for death."

The duel went on with Makail defending everything, acutely waving his sword. Although from Bidellia's vantage point, it appeared King Avar had the upper hand, Makail knew he'd have an opportunity to switch the feet, and when the opportunity came, he'd be ready. The queen snatched Fidelis's eyes; not speaking to keep from interfering with Makail's concentration, lowering her forehead toward many of her fighters, she pointed her open-palmed hand north then motioned west. Puzzled, Fidelis leaned in to whisper, "You want me to pull our men back?"

She nodded her head with her eyes saying, obviously.

"But, my queen, we have them far outnumbered now, we can win with the gargentwans falling back."

The frustrated glare she returned him sparked Fidelis's raxar into motion, and he called back all the Pithlyn men before the queen had to sacrifice anymore.

King Avar simply attacked in continuous motions, spear, sword, spear, sword, pumping like the pistons on train wheels. Makail's ease in swiftness annoyed the king, and those gritted teeth through scowled lips revealed his displeasure. Through the translucent silver semicircle his sword repetitively created, Makail kept Junder in his front sight. To keep the king's sword and spear from scratching him, Makail back pedaled with King Avar's advances, and as the king began to circle, Makail had to follow. Makail didn't want the king to lead the steps, but it had to be that way for now, for Makail's opportunity hadn't opened, but his disaster appeared imminent.

King Avar had strategically circled enough to position Makail's back to Junder. Makail knew he had to get rid of him immediately; Queen Bidellia sensed what would happen if Junder took hold of Makail as she watched intently. King Avar's mouth turned from a strenuous tightness to a wide smile while his arms worked in overdrive. Junder lowered his arms inches from Makail's shoulders, and as though he could see a reflection on King Avar's sword, he rolled back one rotation. King Avar batted his weapons through the empty air when Makail found his feet and jumped to where he could shove his palm into the gargentwans chest, throwing him a hundred yards away in a perfect low parabola. Just as Makail landed, he turned to face his combatant's spear thrusting toward his chest. He quickly fanned his blade and remained on defense, mocking "Your weak attempts." The fierce glare returned, painting King Avar's face with contempt.

Focused on clanking away every swipe and jab, Makail didn't notice a clunking gargentwan charging toward the two. Junder had bounced back quickly, and he wanted revenge. As he neared, King Avar could feel him coming, but he knew on which side Junder fought. What King Avar had not anticipated was Makail rolling to the side when he saw Junder leap through the air, intending to smash Makail into the ground. King Avar turned with his weapons down. Seeing the flying giant, he raised his arms in a reaction to protect himself, but when he raised his arms, his weapons pointed to the sky. Junder saw the king's move and tried rolling his body away, lifting his right shoulder before his chest landed on the tip of King Avar's sword, which continued through his heart. The spear pierced the right side of the gargentwans burly chest, penetrating through his back. And Junder's leap ended on top of the king, who now lain weaponless but breathing, although slightly suffocated.

Makail raised his head with smiling eyes to his queen. She gave him the same response with her own eyes, and they nodded heads together.

Under Junder, the king squirmed free. Once to his feet, he anxiously tried turning the massive being to retrieve his weapons, stuffing his head, shoulders, and arms under the breathless body, seeking enough leverage to push him over. He appeared like an ostrich with his head sunk in the ground. On the other hand, Makail never expected such an obvious and simple opportunity to come. He slowly stepped to King Avar's dirt-encased back, and tapped his shoulder, "Now let's begin our fun."

"You back away at once!" popping his head from the smelly flesh.

"Surrender."

"I will not surrender," a beleaguered king responded. "We are too strong for such a weak escape."

Makail bobbed his head around quickly, figuring the king would remark so stubbornly. Resorting to force became a must. The king's eyes widened, mouth stiff with worry, as Makail tightened his hands around the sword handle. Allowing no time for any reaction, he bashed his clinched hands into King Avar's cheek, drooping him to the ground. Makail straddled the lain chest and froze his eyes to King Avar's. With inquisitively wide eyes and a slanted head, Makail offered the king one more opportunity to say the two words.

With blood beginning to trickle along his lips, the king responded, "You are with no chance of having me surrender."

This obstinance the king perpetually exuded had driven Makail to the brink. Makail knew if he could force King Avar to surrender, everybody of Pithlyn would completely understand his intentions, his meaning. So with a sudden snap of his arm, Makail pressed his left hand against the king's chin, extending his neck. King Avar threw his hands around like a neophyte without a chance of holding off Makail's stone grip. With his right hand, Makail gently clutched his blade, slowly slicing a shallow incision across the neck, keeping care to not make a fatal cut. Despite the king's desperate bellows, Makail had maintained enough concentration to slash a perfect scratch.

"Can you feel the Omnerce hand?" Makail demanded.

King Avar tried lashing out, but as his first word started, the intense pain from his throat became too unbearable. Makail rose to his feet, standing over the impotent king. He slashed away through the kings attire at his chest, stomach, arms, and legs. He'd worked his way down to the king's feet when he jumped back to his original position above the king's chest. As he landed this jump, his sworded arm continued, bring the blade just above King Avar's gashed neck. The king whimpered just loud enough to cause Makail to stop his momentum.

"We're done," he breathlessly admitted. "I cannot defeat you," cringing with every word. "I will have my men retreat, and we will return home at once." "Dymetrice men, gargentwans, and I…surrender."

Rising

"It's over, dearest queen." Makail had made the quick walk to the belly of Lady Leadtheway, who hoisted Bidellia. Through her straight warrior face, he could sense her overwhelming joy but not disbelief. She knew he'd come and force the two armies back, but she did not realize the passion with which he'd fight. Impressed as any, she stared deeply into his eyes. Yes, he's the one she'd always love; he's the one who'd stand up for Pithlyn at times of great acrimony; he's the one her father had molded and sent for her; he's the one who would always return her love.

"No," she answered despite her soul's flooding emotions, "check the south." Makail sharpened his eyes, obviously baffled, wanting her to explain. "See, they're expecting war. When Zyder backs away, this fight's complete." She knew Makail did not need another test to further qualify his devotion to Pithlyn Mass, but she also knew only Makail could work so efficiently to force them out by midday.

Makail peered to the southern mountains, recalling his brief period with Gonko when those very mountains played as a magnificent backdrop to a marvelous dinner. As the sun rose on this morning, it burned a yellow haze from the base brightening on the snowcaps. He turned to his queen and acknowledged, "I'll finish this."

At his words, he fled, reaching his top speed within seconds. Bidellia watched him until her vision could no longer contain the lightning bolt splitting through the grass. Fidelis had returned in time to see Makail force the surrender, and he watched his queen encourage Makail's attempt to heel a southern Zyder force. "I figured I may have been wrong about that guy," he uttered.

"Yes," she agreed, "he's as bright and right as morning's sun."

King Avar had risen to his feet. Pained by a body of razor slits, he announced as loudly as his sore neck would let him, "We'll leave! But your petty traitor of arms will hear from us again," feeling bolder without the presence of the proclaimed traitor.

The queen preferred to not hear from him and wished for him to follow her words, "Just take your men to sea beyond our sand."

The king turned, disrespectfully swiping his hand through the air. When he reached the forest, he met with discombobulated gargentwans making their way back to the front line. He halted their progress, informing them of Tyban and Junder's deaths, and telling them the attempt was over. Even though the gargentwans complained of not letting Makail feel their wrath, King Avar demanded retreat, declaring himself as the leader of this endeavor, and every gargentwan entered this battle understanding King Avar's orders are final. Conceding, the gargentwans helped spread the king's words, glumly guiding all fighters back toward Endefder, where the battle had begun so promisingly, and all the way to their shored ships.

In the southern mountains, Makail had flashed toward Zyder forces, which packed the front of the mountains on a slim floor between them, appearing ready to begin a march to war. As he quickly neared their first line, he jumped to the mountain wall to the west of Zyder's men. From his position, he yelled, "Your king surrenders! Go!" pointing his sword in the direction of Zyder Mass.

Rebellious as the morning sun to a hard sleep, Zyder wouldn't leave. Instead, they launched their throwing pierces in Makail's direction, even though he stood higher on the mountain than any of them could possibly throw. Sensing a collective mulish attitude, Makail rolled his eyes and furiously ran toward the men while commencing boulders to tumble from high on the mountains, proposing they'd leave with such danger falling. To help urge the Zyder army away, Makail bolted through them with stretched arms, flattening them in a domino effect.

As Dymetrice and gargentwan backs dissolved into the woods, Queen Bidellia kept her eyes south while Pithlyn men congratulated fellow survivors, helped the wounded reach the Flowers, and mourned the death of many comrades. Dux banged his way through the forest and into the view of his fellow massmen. "Whooo, thirty-eight," he shrieked. "All in time for breakfast!"

He parked his raxar next to Fidelis, still boasting, "I spilled thirty-eight of those goons and then they all run away." To his own dismay, Fidelis allowed him to continue his ignorant rant. "See, the advantage to having me is pure intimidation. They don't want to mess with anybody associated with me once they see me slaying beasts in every direction from any angle." With his most pompous voice, he finished, "I am warrior beast slayer!" leaving his most intimidating purr to follow his words.

The queen attempted to straighten his view by informing, "Makail provided us this greatest stun."

"Ha," he mocked his queen, "The man is quite

shackled by this point. What would he have anything to do with my great triumph for our great mass?"

"Well, now he fights alone," she pointed toward the beautiful scenery, "to make our stand."

"What is she talking about?" he asked, smacking Fidelis across the chest.

He flopped his shaking head and revealed the Battle of Makail.

Makail's battle halted in the south; while zipping through the falling Zyder troops, he hit a human blockade, two gargentwans. These two had measured the line of Makail's blazing velocity, recognizing precisely how to brace themselves to withstand his impact. When Makail hit the two, they didn't even budge. Instead, they whipped their hands around him, locking him to the grip. Makail's jaw fell a touch, and his eyes widened—more shocked at himself for not heeding the trail ahead and focusing all his attention to flattening Zyder men.

"What," Makail murmured, in complete astonishment, as the gargentwans latched on to both his arms. The boulders beating against the mountain wall resonated louder and louder with the gargentwans standing still, keeping Makail immobile.

"This will be an honorable death," the one stated. "We will die to kill the one Tyban seeks."

"We will die with honor," the other agreed. Each of

the two was completely unaware of Tyban's recent death by Makail's hands, but they knew Tyban had wanted the incredible one dead. Only the incredible one could cause their current surroundings, so they had no doubt, this man they held must die.

The boulders raged down like the snow of an avalanche, and Makail, with all his powers, could do nothing to stop his crumbling mountain, nothing to free himself from the continuous tightening of gargentwan wrenches. He felt powerless, forsaken, and brave. As the heavy mountain chunks neared his end, he wondered if Omnerce came back at him for placing his lips on his daughter's forehead. Makail mumbled, "just a kiss." And the mountain rubble piled high within the abyss floored with Zyder men, two gargentwans, and a Pithlyn hero.

"This must all be part of his impromptu plan of getting rid of Zyder," Fidelis directed his words to the queen while both watched the mountain pieces flutter to the ground. From their view, it looked like steam gliding down the mountain, and once the steam brushed into the bottom, the collapse merely appeared as dust poofing into the air after slapping a hand on an old couch arm. But both knew Makail had devised this incident; he caused the steam and dust.

Queen Bidellia didn't answer him with more than a

nod of her head, knowing his evasive speed would have him far away from any dust and back to her in moments. Moments passed, and as her mental clock recognized he hadn't returned within the same amount of time it took him to leave and create steam, she became frightful. She loved Makail with everything she had, so he had to survive for her. After a few more moments passed, her somber spell intensified.

Fidelis hardly let his eyes gaze away from her face after saying his bit. Her grave expression alerted him, compelling him to ask, "I feel something amiss, what is on your mind to bring such a face?"

"My soul has never felt a fear like this," she explained. Without warning, she clacked her raxar into action.

Startled by her sudden jolt to the south, he attempted to begin chasing her when Dux pulled his own raxar perpendicular to Fidelis. "Are you really planning on following her again?"

"Yes, she needs company for this long endeavor."

"Have you no mind to consider yourself as an unwanted, constant follower? I mean don't you ever think to yourself, maybe she would like to be alone for a few moments?"

"Don't be ridiculous, Dux. There could be danger in this travel. Who knows what she could encounter."

"I believe an immortal queen could possibly handle anything she encounters without a sidekick. You would only make it more difficult for her because she would actually have to watch out for anything that could harm or kill you."

His dumbfounded expression told Dux that he'd won this verbal battle. "She'll be fine," he reassured. "Our royal duty should focus on reorganizing these men and sending them on their beautifully victorious trek home." "By the way, how many of those mudlickers did you end?"

"Mudlickers?"

"Yes, all thirty-eight times I finished a kill, they landed with their mouth open, right on the ground. I had to help the tongue come out a few times, or readjust their face to make sure they had a good taste of Pithlyn mud on their final breath. But overall, they all licked our mud."

Embarrassed by his own lack of fighting, Fidelis jumped back to Dux's idea of their royal duty. "I should certainly say the queen would be satisfied with us by getting all her men on their way home properly."

Dux shook his head, audibly smiling.

Lady Leadtheway bulleted swiftly, like a greyhound, sensing her master's urgency. A trip by raxar from Medeal's Flowers down to the northernmost southern mountain would typically take one full day of maximum distance, but the battle delayed any hope for most raxars to reach the mountains by sundown. For further delay, Queen Bidellia knew Lady would need to stop for water breaks in creeks and rivers they'd pass. Aside from that, she planned to keep the fastest raxar in Pithlyn hustling at top speeds, attempting to reach the steep before darkness invaded, for searching through rubble in a gorge required light.

The queen's mind cluttered with teary thoughts of never feeling Makail's warm breath along her face; never conversing with him again on any topic; and never kissing his lively lips. This pulling emotion surfaced as determination. She had to reach him. If the mountains crushed Makail and did not kill him right away, could he be painfully suffocating to death? With such a hopeful thought, the queen drove forth, stopping for Lady's water every fifty miles or so. On the third water break, the queen dismounted Lady and caressed the raxar's neck. Gazing south, she mentioned, "I wish to press my lips against his kiss." Her chin quivered with the final word as a tear rolled from eye to chin.

For the entire day, Fidelis and Dux followed their own decision by gathering all surviving troops in Endefder, where they witnessed the devastation, and only found several children and four women surviving. Fidelis gave his royal word that Endefder would be restored, starting today. As an army, the thousands repaired broken dwellings, and removed irremediable panels, and debris. Several men who came to battle promised to bring their families so Endefder could live on as defenders of the greatest mass on the sphere.

With daylight closing on Bidellia's mission, the mountains grew taller and taller within her vision, and then she sat upon Lady with the creek-width crevice of a floor covered with chunks of the high mountain. She had arrived. Slipping from the back of her raxar, a delicate scent of stone tinged her nose as dust still lingered from the day's early collision. The overpowering odor of human sweat, flesh, and blood stained her nostrils. Looking upon the scene, she wanted to feel it was a tragic sight, but considering the depleted had invaded her mass, she held far less sympathy for the empty bodies.

Bidellia secured Lady to a tall tree next to a two-foot stream of water. Patting the raxar's rear, she headed into the ruins on a prayer. Repeatedly, she resteadied her footing on the rigid walkway, which consisted of the mountain wall to her right and fallen boulders to her left. She saw hands, feet, and beaten faces. No hand had a bracelet like Makail's; no feet showed bare; no beaten face appeared godly. She continued south, hoping she wouldn't need to attempt moving the hefty boulders—she'd hate to call upon her father after such a morning. Staring south, she could see the final fallen boulder, knowing the sky would darken completely on her walk back to Lady.

Overflowing with forced emotions, wanting to find him alive, she said firmly, "Unknowns in life may bring our happy ends, but what is this?"

"It's how our love extends," a strong voice hollered from below. Frantically searching the stone-flushed ground, she spotted his face, as he continued, "beyond the bounds of loving just for now."

"Makail!" hurrying to his side, "I knew my love would see you through." Her words served as reassurance to herself that she had found the one who'd been sent for her, but also to tell Makail that because she loves him, he can survive anything.

"And like I said, I do survive for you." His eyes flexed from Bidellia's to the boulders that once covered his entire being. The two stood atop one layer of boulders while pinched between the second layer. Although it only took him a few moments to find his way from the bottom of the rubble to standing on it all, he couldn't believe he'd slithered away unscathed. He'd stared at his hands, arms, and legs, not a single scratch. He dabbed his fingers all over his face, not feeling any sign of a mark. What happened? he wondered. Why hadn't the mountain crushed him to his death as it did so many others in the abyss? Unsure, he'd tightened his sword in hand and grazed it across is bicep with no reaction, so he'd ripped it across the same line, nothing. He'd gripped the sword with both hands, holding the handle away from him with the sharp tip aimed toward him. As he'd thrust it in for kill, he only threw himself back a small hop. Completely fuddled, he'd run a short distance up the mountain and jumped to a fall, crashing hard on the boulders beneath him—not a scratch. Adrenaline had flowed, excitement had teased, Makail torched his way to the mountain's summit and leaped for the ruinous base with arms flapping, legs jolting. When he'd hit the bottom, his stomach stuck, feeling no pain. He could not be harmed! He sat in the spot where Bidellia had found him for the remaining day, wondering how this could be possible.

Noticing his bewilderment and disbelief, Bidellia explained, "You're now immortal as the gods endow because my love of life will never die."

Grabbing her hands from her side, he held them delicately, feeling their softness. He gazed deep into her eyes, knowing how much she loved him and how much he'd always love her. He described, "I felt my end when mountains fell from high; instead," his face transformed from stern to elated, "you're keeping me beneath your brow."

Chapter 23

Dropping her hands from him, she wrapped her arms over his neck, pulling herself close to his body. "Forever," she encouraged with a smile, before perking up her eyes and adding, "if you wish eternal bliss."

"Eternal bliss," he repeated, nodding his head, "we'll start it with a kiss." She leaned up to him, wanting the kiss he'd indicated. Makail lowered his face a touch to touch her lips with his.

Bidellia, despite not wanting to stop, ducked her head back to demand, "We'll let forever be our strongest vow, as I will always hold my love," maintaining warm eye contact, she finished "Makail."

Bowing his head, he eyed his parents' bracelets once more. He smiled, knowing the meaning of these bracelets. He unclasped the one from his right wrist, and gently grabbed the queen's soft, warm left hand. A tear brimmed within her eye as Makail wrapped his mother's bracelet around his love's wrist. "And we shall hold the greatest storytale."

Poetic Bidellia
An Appendix

Chapter 4

For far too many years, I've been alone,
Without a man to love and comfort me,
And as I've sat upon the highest throne,
I've never loved. Now think, how could this be?
It's true, my love is vast for all the men,
The women, and the children of our land,
Yet men won't dare to share my love. So then,
If Pithlyn holds no man to grasp my hand,
I'll search afar, but first, where shall I turn?
Indiffrin, Zyder, Glaci, not a chance!
Dymetrice, as a whole, I'd rather burn,
But Favally just might be worth a glance.
  In all the land, there must be one with whom
  I'd share this life forever set to bloom.

Chapter 8

He stared and noticed her from foot to face.
She held the stature of a goddess' grace
With slender features arms and legs and waist.
The splendor of her eyes could ease a gaze—
Blue eyes to light a flameless room ablaze,
And blondest hair, which kept her neck encased
Then floating to the mid of back in waves.
Her smile, her shining smile with lips he craves
To frame the whitest teeth the sun's embraced,
Which cause the smile to melt the soul of all.
Her softest, fairest skin could never pall—
Poetic beauty of the finest taste.
   She holds the beauty one could not digest,
   As she's perfection at perfection's best.

Chapter 9 (Makail's soliloquy)

At once, I hear the voices of my past.
My parents said this queen will keep me safe,
Yet she confines me to this wretched hole,
Surrounding me with wretched souls of men,
And only for innate Dymetrice roots?
This Queen Bidellia, the immortal queen,

Poetic Bidellia

Who thrust this filth on me, a loathsome rule,
May never understand the strength I hold,
As my protection spans to boundless spans
Yet she deduces me to sleep with rats
When I could bring her glory's greatest gift.
So why'd she throw me to this tiny cell
Without a chance to prove goodwill to her?
For I have come to seek the ways of life
On Pithlyn Mass, a mass my soul has felt
To be my destined home, rejoice, and grace.
I've come to Pithlyn not to cause ado
But put to rest the unrests of the past.
Oh, Queen Bidellia never gave a chance,
And since she's summoned someone such a scorn,
I'm left to dwell in dwellings all alone,
So now my rage is for the queen's return,
Or once again, how could she keep me safe?
Immortal queen, my parents' last request.
A lovely queen, heartbreaking queen, indeed.
A kind and loving queen to meet the eye.
When wrath subsides and I can find my head,
It may be true that I'm in love, Makail.

Appendix

Chapters 6, 8, and 9

I've slept so well, but morning comes too soon.
Morn, when the sun returns, we'll take our ride.
It's such a truth! I ought to wake the moon;
Next rise of sun will set my soul aglide,
Let first, today: the people need our view.
Oh, search the huts. We've found the man of fault.
Verboten Faults, no guest is welcomed through.
Eschew the man! Before the dusk, we halt.
My yes, I love the ones who walk my grass,
And all these men have quivered at my thumb.
Kill? Purge this man, I'm queen of Pithlyn Mass
As he's no more than some Dymetrice scum.
I'll have the man escorted to the bleak.
Lone soul I am with most of man so meek.

Chapter 10

Dymetrice, cold and dark without a soul,
Or not a kinder soul to reach with care,
And Zyder differs none, accepting dole
While praising high before Dymetrice air.
But Favally should have the one who's right.
Oh, now the surest queen is left unsure.

I know I'll sleep alone again tonight.
She speaks: the perfect man survives for her.
He lives today, so let us search and find,
And find we shall; He walks the present soil.
In Favally, the stars shall shine aligned.
To find him we must rest to bear our moil.
    I'm set. Despite our lack of luck so far,
      He's there; he's here; the gods have seen my star.

Chapter 11

In Favally, the queen had troubles still.
No man stood bold enough to rise with grit,
For each had acted as they always will.
This showed her soul a need to quickly quit,
And yet, her journey formed a long retreat
With gawking men who stare and shy away
Then kiss the footprints of her stepping feet.
Thus, on a day when skies began to gray,
She told Fidelis time had come to leave.
Dejected, Queen Bidellia searched above,
And leaving, wondered who the gods believe
To be the one surviving as her love.
    An empty journey ended all for naught;
      Arriving home, she lingered deep in thought.

Chapter 12

Oh, gods above, reveal my man for life,
For all I've faced have faded all too soon.
My soul is sinking, swapping hope for strife
Now, show me to the man who hums the tune
And silence to the ones who wrongly shout!
My gods, this can't be who you've brought for me,
For he's not rising to respect my clout.
Perhaps a duel proves the petty plea?
Then we shall clash our swords at mountain's base.
We make our start to see the swiftest scud.
Hold nothing back, for no one scathes this face!
If only he were not Dymetrice blood,
   At ease, I may forever be forlorn.
   Unless my love's in this Dymetrice born.

Chapter 13

You're not an easy man for me to know
You're born Dymetrice, now you're Pithlyn's pick.
You run much faster than the wind can blow;
You're sword is graceful, moving all too quick;
And then, you blare through air without a care.
Now, what's a fuddled queen to make of this?

Do speak the truth and tell why you are rare.
And you survived for everlasting bliss.
I ought to share with you some tales of past,
But first, you must have more to share on things.
The humming tunes, are those the spells you cast?
The song was beautiful, as he who sings.
    You still have very much to prove, Makail,
    But there's a chance that you're my storytale.

Chapters 13 and 14

A storytale holds more than stories told,
But not a tale for others' disbelief.
It's when a man or woman finds the gold
Within a soul to keep through time not brief.
In Pithlyn, every soul will cherish theirs.
I took him for a night. No further bid,
For he had shown most everything he bares.
Makail, whatever did you sleep amid?
You're strange indeed, but I will also say,
No god or goddess ever fancied such.
I've never met a man who acts your way
With all your strengths and nerve yet gentle touch.
    You bleed the purest blood of Pithlyn blue
    So I may see myself to cherish you.

Chapter 14

About my past, what would you like to hear?
I'm queen and Living Goddess for the live.
With words, I grant men courage, never fear
I'll talk; men battle with their souls that thrive.
In Favally, we won while sharing grass;
I've marched my troops across the Clatter Crest
To battle gargentwans of Glaci Mass
And win allegiance from the quasi quest.
To Zyder Mass, we crunched them ledge to ledge,
Yet still they're loyal to the north command
Where land, from us, is pinched, declines from edge,
As God of Peace had clinched and ripped the land.
   And now, we have the Threatle Gap to keep
   Dymetrice distant—they're our crudest creep.

Chapter 14

You're charming, like a child who praises me,
But in a manly way as nature's gleam.
You're not a child, that's very plain to see;
It's like the gods have sent you from a dream.
Your chest is of the mountains with a beat.
Your eyes are of the leafless trees with snow.

Your scent is of a manly smell, but sweet.
Your sweetness deepens where my love may grow.
I can't subject myself to loving yet,
For ugly endings come when moving fast,
Which turn a lovely love to soon regret,
So tell of coming here, or recent past.
   Then on this path, you did not end the men?
   Do sing our praise, we're off to war again.

Chapter 14 and 15

It's better if you leave at once, Makail.
The trouble here is they are coming, Leave!
Fidelis, bring me Dux; we must prevail.
This time we have is but a quick reprieve
Before the storms of masses raid the east.
Be calm, the gargentwans have bent on us
Because Makail defeated two. At least,
They'll start to fight from they're defeat, and thus,
They'll force their forces from Dymetrice Wall.
We must remain to hope Dymetrice stays
Or else too many Pithlyn men will fall
Such claims describe a daunting, haunting haze
   Makail pumps Pithlyn blood; the flowers tell.
   Prepare the troops and bang the battle bell.

Appendix

Chapter 15 and 17

At once, this meeting here is now adjourned.
I'll find Makail with help from gods above.
Unproven love can never be returned.
The love of Pithlyn Mass would prove your love.
He's kind to me, yet bold and daring too.
You know I'd never love the traitor kind.
Now there's a massive fleet we must subdue,
And even worse if all of them combined.
Dymetrice, Glaci, even Zyder might
Join force and form a legion vast as all.
We'll send our wave due east where we will fight
The largest beast, so take your best and stall
    No more, for war is soon; my men have heft
    To battle on till all the opps have left.

Chapter 17

We'll fight for Pithlyn's breath, which gives to most
The courage bold enough to fight enraged.
So let us battle best at eastern coast
And slay the beast without our deaths so staged!
How might we win, and what's the Pithlyn toll?
Do let our steel exceed the steel of foes.

Great gods must guard my every Pithlyn soul.
Makail, we cannot win unless he goes.
My feelings feel like you are very wrong,
But you've been fair, and I will trust in you.
With morrow's morning, we will take our strong
To clash until triumphant through and through.
   The stars shine brightly, like they're Omnerce eyes,
   Which say, we'll never meet with our demise.

Chapter 18

Our rival haunts our east, much like the past,
But we've prepared for them with haste and vim.
Now for this final time we stand so massed,
I'll say that even if our hope is grim,
We can't back down; defending Pithlyn Mass
Is most of all to all of those alive.
We'll fight with vigor, love, and souls of brass,
And gods above will see our Pithlyn thrive.
The gargentwans will bring their bladed spheres;
Poor Zyder always has their throwing pierce;
We know Dymetrice arms themselves with spears.
A massive squall, but we will keep it fierce,
   As this attack will forge Endefder first,
   So we will fight with gods; our foe is cursed.

Appendix

Chapter 18

Oh, what's the worry of your mind tonight?
We've only passed through trails for days of one.
I'd bid Makail to ride with us and fight,
For he's of gods—Isnelle and Jivin's son.
On what a whim, we've weld him with the walls.
It's you and I, my Lady Leadtheway,
So let us travel harsh while Omnerce calls!
You're better not to let your judgment sway.
(The rest of this is not in the book)

Chapters 20 and 21

Attention, thank you all for coming here
And standing ready to protect our mass.
Tomorrow, we will set aside the fear
To fight with courage, letting no man pass!
We stand tonight with twenty thousand strong;
We fight so soon with strength of all behind,
And gods will bless our battle cries with song,
Defeating foe while fighting intertwined
With gods who'll lead us to a gloried end.
So rest tonight, obtain your strength to fight.
You must be glad he had a sword to lend.

You need not lie; this sword should serve you right.
　It's sturdy with a fighter's soul entrenched.
　We're under raid! No time for acting blenched!

Chapters 21 and 22

　They've hit Endefder! Omnerce speaks to me.
　You know my father never leads astray.
　Yes, such a battle though deserves no glee.
　Dymetrice looms; they've pounced to pound their
　　　prey.
　Your body ever rests with Pithlyn Mass,
　But Omnerce honors soul in Gracen's light
　Your body ever rests with Pithlyn Mass,
　But Omnerce honors soul in Gracen's light
　Your body ever rests with Pithlyn Mass,
　But Omnerce honors soul in Gracen's light
　Your body ever rests with Pithlyn Mass,
　But Omnerce honors soul in Gracen's light
　　This faulty fleeting flail of hope I had
　　Has caused the many deaths we see; it's sad.

Chapters 22 and 23

Bidellia:
I give you me, let Omnerce choose the rest.

283

My Pithlyn vows surrender, ending drear.
You'll fight for Pithlyn Pride with passion's best
As courage has become your former fear.
My love, he's not a coward; let him soar.
He's merely trouncing forces with his feet.
No, check the south; see, they're expecting war.
When Zyder backs away, this fight's complete.
Yes, he's as bright and right as morning's sun.
Just take your men to sea beyond our sand.
Makail provided us this greatest stun,
And now he fights alone to make our stand.
   My soul has never felt a fear like this.
   I wish to press my lips against his kiss.

Makail:
She lies. I give you me as foe in quest,
For Pithlyn never will surrender here.
I'll fight with fear inside my beating chest,
For fear of fears is losing you, my dear,
My love, my love, and they've come back for more.
For Pithlyn, you surrender now! Retreat!
Then see my parents, if it weren't for Core.
My kin would rather see you meet defeat.
Surrender yet? I'd hate to end the one
Who took my parents' lives. You'll never land.
Your weak attempts. Now aren't we having fun.

Surrender. Can you feel the Omnerce hand?
It's over, dearest queen. I'll finish this.
Your king surrenders! Go! What, just a kiss.

Chapter 23

Unknowns in life may bring our happy ends,
But what is this? It's how our love extends
Beyond the bounds of loving just for now.
Makail! I knew my love would see you through.
And like I said, I do survive for you.
You're now immortal as the gods endow
Because my love of life will never die.
I felt my end when mountains fell from high;
Instead, you're keeping me beneath your brow.
Forever, if you wish eternal bliss
Eternal bliss, we'll start it with a kiss.
So let forever be our strongest vow,
   As I will always hold my love, Makail.
   And we shall hold the greatest storytale.

Makail to Bidellia in Chapter 13

In brief, my parents lived on Pithlyn soil.
The gods had granted them uncommon gifts
To help protect the Pithlyn plains and hills.

Appendix

The gifts could flatten mountains, wave the deep,
Ablaze a forest, tip the trees, outfight
A legion, run and jump like nothing else,
And scale to peaks of any mountain top.
But when my mother knew I turned inside
She wanted all the feuding gone and done.
So she, and with my father, found a home:
Dymetrice, near the king to keep at peace
With hopes to make as friends with those they'd
    doomed.
It started with success, but others talked;
The next in line as king, now King Avar,
Had known the former plot to raze the reign.
His foremost task was ending both their lives.
My parents came aware of this and sent
Me off to live in Quintix Valley's woods,
As they complied with kingly orders dread.
You see now, only cowards flee from death,
And only cowards let their children die.
That's why they sent me there to hone my skills
Until I grew in strength enough to find
The highest queen in all the sphere abroad:
A tougher task, but I survived for you.

About the Author

Kevin Jackson

Although this is the first book of mine available to the public, I have written several other novels, novellas, and short stories. My prized work, without winning anything for it, remains my collection of sonnets, which has surpassed the number within Shakespeare's collection.

I'm currently working on my next book, which I've outlined as a trilogy, taking place between a fantasy world and a small mid-Michigan city. I've implemented a similar writing style as you saw woven throughout this book, and I hope you will enjoy it moreso than you have *Storytale.*

If you took the time to view the preceding appendix, you have seen every syllable to roll off Queen Bidellia's tongue. Every word she speaks glides through meters of iambs, and this specific format is iambic pentameter. You will also note a consistent rhyme scheme throughout her words.

Thank you for reading my book, and if you have any comments, or would like to connect with me, you may do so on Facebook, where I have a personal page.

Proof